Focused on capturing elusive facts . . .

Emily hadn't considered her safety. Her steps slowed as she sensed another's presence. Security lights illuminated the darkness, but only within their radius. To her left, like a thick blue gel, the pool cast a spooky glow.

Emily took a deep breath. Now wasn't the time to give into fear. She and Dillon were close to an answer. She knew it.

She jerked her attention forward, expecting to see someone standing in the path. Nothing. The evening silence thickened until all she heard was the sound of her own breathing. *Get moving, you dope. You're an open target standing in the light.*

The stone walkway beckoned her to safety. Emily started forward. Movement in the shadows brought her to a dead halt. She strained to see through the darkness.

The shadow moved.

Books by Regina Tittel

Abandoned Hearts

Abandoned Hearts Study Guide

Unexpected Kiss

Coveted Bride

Cherished Stranger

Love for Lenore
historical short story - ebook

Rivalry & Romance
historical short story

Coming Titles by Regina Tittel

Four Times a Charm
In Warsaw MO series
(historical short story)

Conveniently Yours
After the Vows series vol. 1

Devoted Mission

Regina Tittel

The Ozark Durham Series vol. 5

DEVOTED MISSION

Published by Hawse Pipe Ministries
Copyright © 2014 by Regina Tittel
Cover design by Regina Tittel
Edited by Angela Breidenbach

All Scripture quotations are taken from the King James Version.

ISBN-10: 0988900254
ISBN-13: 978-0-9889002-5-7

Regina Tittel wrote Devoted Mission to bring awareness to the spiritual needs of the Kurdish people both stateside and abroad. And to convey the spiritual side of this world and the power of prayer we have through our Lord, Jesus Christ.

For we wrestle not against flesh and blood, but against principalities, against powers, against the rulers of the darkness of this world, against spiritual wickedness in high places.

–Ephesians 6:12

Then saith he unto his disciples, The harvest truly is plenteous, but the labourers are few; Pray ye therefore the Lord of the harvest, that he will send forth labourers into his harvest.

–Matthew 9:37-38

Thank you, Gin, for your sacrifice for God's kingdom.
May you always be blessed.

Thank you Jerad, and our beautiful children who
constantly encourage me.

I also must thank,
Cortland, for titling this book
Jeni, for standing shoulder to shoulder with me in
this battle
Karen, for informing me about baseball games (since
I'm clueless!)
Laura, for sharing your journey in adoption with me
And to all those working with the Kurds.

Always, thank you, Jesus.

Chapter One

November

"Can you hear me?" Emily Durham's throat tightened. A tingling sensation, like a thousand little spiders, crawled up the back of her neck. Something wasn't right. Deer season ended two days ago. Why was this man still here?

A cold wind rattled the few dry leaves that clung to parent limbs. Emily blinked against a lock of hair that blew across her face and shivered. The hunter's lack of response spiked the hair on her arms despite layers of clothing. His slack jaw made him appear more dead than alive. She eased back into the brush, cringing as branches scraped against the nylon fabric of her coat and strained to see past the trees.

Nothing moved. Nothing made a sound—including the man slumped on the ground.

Back in the states for a week, yet it felt as if she were still in an overseas war-torn country. Only this time she didn't have a guide. She wasn't on a mission trip. And no one knew where she was.

Her breath turned shallow as her heart hammered against her ribs. *Jesus, You've led me this far. Help me know what to do next.* Before her, lay an injured man. Behind, stretched the deer trail leading back to the cabin. Dread wrapped around her like a shroud.

Emily held the branches back and stepped lightly to avoid snapping twigs. While her head warned, *get away*, her heart couldn't leave the man alone.

She dropped to her knees beside the lifeless form. A shudder coursed up her spine. Her gaze trailed from the man's pale face to a semi-dry, dark smear staining the front of his orange vest. Her breath caught in her throat. What started out as a reminiscent walk through the woods turned into a nightmare.

"Please, Jesus, let him be alive." She pressed her fingers against his bearded throat and held her breath.

Nothing.

Not willing to accept no for an answer, she moved her fingers and pressed tighter. Her eyes squeezed tight as her mouth moved in a fervent prayer.

A faint pulse thrummed against her skin. Emily exhaled in relief. "Thank you, Jesus." She shed her winter coat and laid it over the man, tucking it around him the best she could. "I'm not leaving you. I'll be right back."

Her attention caught on a rifle as she turned to leave. Had the hunter walked this far then dropped his gun from exertion? She picked it up by the fore stock and positioned it across his lap, pointing the muzzle away from the path. "Just in case."

Emily sprinted through the woods, dodging trees and briary patches that could slow her down. Haunting worries imprisoned her thoughts. What if she took too long and he died before she returned? What if he had children wondering why their daddy hadn't come home?

What if she came back to find the gun pointed at her?

She stumbled but caught her balance before hitting the forest floor. Her heart argued the man wasn't the threat. But why the caution? She wouldn't brush it off to a wild imagination. Years spent as a missionary, often surrounded by God's enemies, had taught Emily to follow her instinct. And that trust saved her life more times than her family would ever know.

Ten minutes later her brother's cabin came into view. Although empty, save for her few belongings, the cabin hid a shed on the other side.

Emily halted beside the house and strained to catch her wind. Cold air burned her lungs more than the exertion. Her breath made bursts of white clouds as Emily ignored the stitch in her side and hurried forward. She slipped her key into the master lock of the shed and threw open the door. Ethan's old four-wheeler. A gas can set against the wall. Fuel sloshed inside. A gallon was all she'd need. A couple hard thrusts of the throttle, and the motor roared to life. Emily rushed back down the path.

The wind created by the increased speed chilled through her thin layers of cotton. Each time the trail narrowed and caused she veered off course, a harsh shiver racked her body. With her thoughts on the injured man, she regretted not grabbing another coat.

Emily maneuvered around another patch of scrub. *I'm taking too long. What if he dies?*

The orange color of the hunter's vest came within view. She drew the ATV as close as she could, hoping the sound of the motor would stir him.

He didn't move.

"Sir, I'm going to move you." Whether he could hear or not, she felt better talking out loud. The rifle lay untouched. Emily checked its safety then positioned it across the front rack of the ATV. From his uninjured side, she slipped the man's arm across her shoulders and shoved her feet against the forest floor. The man moaned and rolled his head to the side. Relief bubbled through her chest.

Leaning back against the tree for support, Emily's legs shook as her tightened muscles strained to bring them to a stance. He moaned again.

"I'm so sorry, but you have to get to a doctor." Bark scraped against her coat releasing the smell of broken fungi. She forced air out her nose to ward off the urge to sneeze. The sharp movement might send them both to the ground.

"Wha'?" Pain laced the man's voice, but at least he was alert.

"I'm helping you." She took a deep breath then steadied his weight against hers. "Can you see the four-wheeler? You have to help me get you there."

He raised his head only to drop it against hers like a weight. "No stren'."

She inhaled and exhaled heavily. Without his help, she may as well have been moving a bear. With the inside of her foot, she shoved his forward then took a step of her own. Stopping to breathe in enough stamina for their next move, Emily repeated the steps until they reached the ATV.

***

At the hospital with her parents on either side, Emily stared as the helicopter whisked the injured man into the air. Her body felt cold and numb. Shocked.

She'd witnessed enough injuries overseas why did this incident bother her?

As if reading her thoughts, her stepmother, Ann, squeezed her arm. "You weren't expecting this. Not here at home."

If it weren't for her parents stopping by, Emily might still be struggling to get the hunter into the truck.

Her dad had driven while her step-mom followed in their car. Emily helped steady the man over the jolts of the road. His eyes opened once, revealing a deep hazel dark with pain. She doubted he saw anything.

"They'll be able to do more for him in the city than they could here." Her dad wrapped his arm around her and squeezed.

"What about his family?" This wasn't supposed to be part of her furlough. Emotions Emily struggled to control slipped out in confusion. "I've never appreciated my size until now."

She covered her eyes and sniffed. "I couldn't have helped him if I'd been as small as you, Mom."

Emily massaged her neck to relieve the pain and tension. The man had been heavy. Not that he seemed overweight, just taller than her and solid.

She shuddered as his wound replayed in her mind. The conservation land butted up against her family's farm. Although open to public hunting, they rarely had anyone that far in—which made the whole situation strange. Who had fired the stray bullet?

***

Six months later …

Emily adjusted the strap of her sandal and smoothed her skirt. The atmosphere of the office, although expensive, emitted welcomed warmth. Cherry bookcases stretched to the white paneled ceiling, enveloped in decorative molding and offset by moss colored walls. A stylish rug of interlocking circles and squares overlaid the hardwood floor. The retro carpet mixed with the elegant shelving reflected an open mind. A mind willing to take risks and explore new possibilities.

The shelves held books and unique, twisted designs of brass, copper, and iron. Her possible new employer ran a lighting company, but the pieces appeared more artful in form.

The door opened an inch. A man's voice spoke patiently to his listener. "You know you're asking me to do that during business hours. It'll have to wait until this evening." Silence followed by feet stomping away.

"I'm Robert Brewington." A man entered and held out his hand. "Just Robert, no mister."

Emily stood, surprised to see his height envelope hers by a good three inches, and shook his hand. "Emily Durham, no mister to my name either." The immediate ease she felt with him over the phone was present in person as well.

The man's features reminded Emily of the hunter she'd found in the woods, minus the beard. She held her breath and searched his eyes before he turned. Emily's anticipation didn't last long. The man from the woods had hazel eyes. Mr. Brewington's were brown. Disappointment replaced the momentary hope. Why did she keep looking for someone who might not have survived?

"Have a seat, please." Robert picked up her resume and sat on the edge of the desk. "I've looked over the application you faxed. I already knew you'd be a good fit from the phone interview, and your experience overseas should give you a balanced understanding of the children's needs.

"This convention I'm attending is only for a week, but I'll probably be gone for two with meetings and the like. Since the business picked up, I fly out usually every month and from there schedule meetings with other companies, distributors, etc. We have an over-zealous sales marketer, and I admit, I'm just as bad."

He paused and scratched his head. "I know you mentioned it on the phone, but how long did you say you have left before you return to the mission field?"

"Four months."

"Good. Without the kids' mother here I was afraid I'd have to put them through summer school. School alone is hard enough on my daughter. I didn't want her to suffer through vacation as well."

Emily's curiosity piqued. Why didn't his wife step in? During Emily's interview, Robert briefly discussed his adopted children and estranged wife, but surely the woman still cared for the children.

A framed photograph on the desk showed a pretty blonde poised beside Robert. The woman looked immaculate. Her face as perfect as if the photo had been airbrushed, not a stray-a-way hair on her head, and French manicured nails graced the hand on her husband's arm.

"And if they give you too much trouble, my brother will be here to give you a hand."

"Who?" She focused her attention, a little too late. Had Robert said she'd be sharing a house with his brother? He'd better be married.

Robert chuckled. "You've got that deer-in-the-headlights look. My brother, Dillon, lives in the guesthouse and works out of the shop." He stood and motioned her to follow. The man had a constant flow of energy about him.

Outside in the back yard, he pointed across the lawn. "See the house and shop. He won't be far should you need him. And I'm sure the kids will want to interrupt him plenty." Robert turned serious. "Let them. They'll need it. And whether Dillon thinks so or not, he does too."

Emily stared at the immaculate property. Situated at the back of a dead-end lane, the elegant estate boasted a fence on both sides then extended to an open field bordered by trees. A perfect retreat from the rush of city life.

"Dillon keeps mostly to himself designing our top lighting products." He turned back to the house. "Come on. Let me introduce you to my kids."

Once inside, the phone rang from the direction of the office. "Sorry. I need to see to that. Why don't you meet Dillon instead? Just make yourself at home, no need to knock." Robert ushered her outside again and toward the shop.

Meet his brother? By herself?

Emily followed the stone walkway that trailed through the yard, weaving around tightly controlled gardens of shrubs and flowers. She tossed her head back and glanced at the sky, her long hair brushing against her back. "Thank you, God. The last part of my furlough will feel like the retreat it's supposed to be."

The path separated. Emily turned away from the guesthouse and strolled toward the handsome board and bat building. Visible through the open windows and door, welding equipment and shards of metal littered the floor near the center while lighting fixtures lined shelves along the wall. Like dad's barn and

Ethan's woodworking shed, it was a man's domain. However, this building possessed a different smell than what memory served her of home. Hot metal and solder tickled her nose. She maneuvered around boxes of glass bulbs and wiring. "Hello-o-o."

A man looked up from leaning over a worktable. Huge eyes blinked behind protruding, telescope-like lenses that hung over heavy frames. Emily stopped in her tracks. If Mr. Magoo wore glasses—A giggle bubbled up in her throat. She coughed and covered her mouth with her hand. There was nothing she could do to hide the amusement in her eyes.

The man cocked his head to the side and scratched his temple with a forefinger. Emily tightened the muscles in her face, but they weren't strong enough to combat his cartoon-like appearance. Spurts of laughter tumbled past her lips.

With a swift movement of his hand, he swiped the glasses off his face. "Can I help you?"

Uh oh! If this was Dillon Brewington, they definitely weren't off to a good start.

Chapter Two

"I'm Emily Durham." Emily motioned toward the house. The corner of her mouth twitched as she tried to stifle a smile. "The nanny your brother hired."

A shadow fell over the man's face. A handsome, sturdy face, somewhat like his brother's but different. A bead of sweat trickled in an uneven pattern down Dillon's forehead between his brows. He swiped the bridge of his nose against his sleeve.

Had she made a mistake? "I assumed he was your brother. Aren't you Dillon?"

"Yeah, I'm Dillon." His chest rose and fell as he stared. Then he glanced back at the table as if it would save him. "Look, I have work to do. It was nice meeting you."

She gave a moment to Dillon's retreating back, then shrugged. One brother a risk taker, the other an artist.

Near the door a large dome of blown glass snatched her attention. The freckled rust and burgundy pattern blended out from a yellow top and ended with a slight wave of curls at the base. She couldn't resist resting on her heels to touch the beautiful creation.

"Don't!"

"I'm not a child. I had no intention of picking it up—I just wanted to feel it." The smooth, cool surface was as beautiful to touch as to look upon. "This is incredible."

Dillon lifted Emily's hand from the artwork, bringing her to a stance. "Thank you." As if embarrassed, he quickly dropped her hand like a piece of hot metal.

His shy actions lit Emily's curiosity. Was he uncomfortable around everyone, or just her? She wished he would look back so she could study his eyes. Were they green or hazel? He hadn't held her gaze long enough to reveal their color.

Dillon pointed to the glass. "I made that in a friend's studio. It can't be duplicated." He gestured her toward the door.

Entranced by his ability and the shelves full of art she wanted to examine, Emily wasn't ready to leave.. "What is it for? Are you working on it now?"

His mouth formed a tight line while she fought the urge to smile. He didn't like her intrusion, but how could she hide her enthusiasm? Wasn't he used to praise? His uptight actions intrigued her even more.

"I'm working on something else at the moment. Now if you'll excuse me."

She glided out the door but like a mischievous imp, looked over her shoulder. "Sure, but I'll be back."

As she strolled along the path toward the house, her conscious shamed her for teasing the poor man. Perhaps she should control her interest in his work. Her mind switched gears from his talent to his appearance. He looked like his brother Robert, but possessed a completely different personality.

The door opened as Emily approached the house. "How'd it go?"

She raised an eyebrow at Robert. "That smirk tells me you already know."

Her employer's mouth stretched into a smile as he motioned her to follow.

"Are you going to explain why you didn't go with me?"

"The phone rang, remember?"

Emily dropped the subject. She wanted the job too much to demand an answer for which she already knew. Brother ribbing brother.

Robert led her through the kitchen. A dark haired woman wearing an apron smiled warmly before turning back to the sink. Perhaps, the hired cook? Emily looked forward to meeting her.

The Brewington home held something to catch her eye at every turn. They retraced their steps toward the front entrance, passed through the sitting ,room with its beamed ceiling and came to the curved stairs in the foyer. She committed the tour to memory. This would be the short-term employment that helped pay her next mission trip.

"I've already told you about my son from your first interview, but here's a bit more." Robert's voice dropped to a whisper. "Not long after his birth, his mother died of malaria then six years later his dad died of aids."

Emily had encountered similar cases when she'd visited orphanages in the boy's home country of Africa.

Soon they were at the first room. The door swung open. "Dad! Can you play ball now?" He paused then shared a bright smile with Emily. "Hullo." He reached his hand to her hair. "Very pretty. What color is it?"

Emily drew a lock in front of her face. "My mom always called it strawberry blonde."

"Jabali. This is Emily, the nanny I hired." The boy continued to smile. "She'll stay here while I'm at the convention."

Jabali's smiled faltered. He dropped his eyes to the floor then in a smaller voice asked again. "Can we play ball?"

"I promised you, didn't I?" Fatherly love filled Robert's voice. "We'll play this afternoon."

The boy jerked his head up and took Emily's hand. "I'm ten, how old are you?"

Robert coughed into his hand and struggled to speak. Emily waved him off. "I don't mind telling. I'm thirty-three."

"Em-i-ly. I like to say your name."

"Thank you," her heart melting already. "Can you show me your room? Are those signed baseballs?"

He smiled widely and pulled her toward a shelf near his bed. The next few minutes Emily learned more about baseball than she'd ever known. The child had certainly been immersed into an all-time favorite American sport.

"How far is the Cardinal's stadium from here?"

Robert answered. "Only about thirty minutes. We never missed a game last year, did we son?" Their attachment to one another was evident and genuine. It seemed they'd made a natural adaption to the role of father and son.

"Are you ever coming to see my room?" A surly twelve-year-old stood at the door's entrance. Her speech still thick with a Ukrainian accent.

"We were just coming, Rhysa."

Unlike Jabali's blue walls, Rhysa's were all white. She pointed to a dresser. "I want to move that over against the other wall and change things around, but Dad is making me wait until tonight."

Emily nodded in understanding. Rhysa must have been the one he'd spoken to before entering the office. She obviously didn't like waiting to get her way. She was tall for twelve years and sturdy. Her blonde hair was worn in a tight ponytail, accenting her strong, yet symmetric face. Emily pictured her with a smile and saw the beauty her frown kept masked.

"Rhysa, this is the nanny I hired for the summer. Say hello to Emily."

Emily held out her hand. "It's nice to meet you, Rhysa."

The girl ignored the offered handshake and shrugged. "We don't have to be friends. It's not like anyone sticks around."

***

Sweat trickled down the back of Dillon's shirt. What was his brother thinking? Dillon knew they needed a nanny, but he'd expected to meet a sweet, grandma figure or at the very least, a strict schoolmarm.

Certainly not someone like Emily.

There was something familiar about the strawberry blonde. Dillon searched his thoughts. He pictured her appealing face in all the places he frequented. Nothing matched.

What did it matter anyway?

He lit the torch and resumed his work. Still, not placing her face irritated him. The distraction would only cause him to err and ruin everything he'd achieved that morning. He shoved Emily's face from his mind and focused on the whoosh of the acetylene.

As if Dillon's senses needed the change, her face wasn't the familiar memory—it was her voice.

Why would he remember someone's voice?

The heated brass tubing slipped from his gloved hands and clanked to the floor. He blew a long breath between his teeth. He couldn't risk getting behind schedule. The shipment for Brewington's Lighting and Displays latest design was due by the end of the week.

"So what did you think?"

Dillon turned toward the door to his brother. "I think you're nuts. You know I've got a tight deadline and you hire the most beautiful one out there."

"No." Robert dragged out the word and tapped his fingers on both hands together. "I hired the most qualified."

Dillon reached for the tubing. "I doubt you interviewed anyone else."

"I'll only be gone a couple of weeks. Then I'll be here to interact with her." His tone intimated it would be cause for jealousy.

Dillon knew Robert took his marriage too seriously for that. It was just a ruse to propel him on board. "Good. I don't need the distraction."

"Yes, you do. This box you live in," Robert held his palm out toward the shop's interior, "isn't healthy. Forget your past and move on."

Dillon raised a shoulder toward his ear and cringed. Their playful banter just took a personal hit. Why did Robert think Dillon's choice to submerge himself in work tied to a couple of failed relationships? It was a decade old argument. He smirked, "You need new material. You've grown stale."

Robert shook his head and withheld comment. Even without the last word, he sauntered away in confidence. Probably certain he was still in the winning.

The whole situation made Dillon uncomfortable.

Since the Brewington business' growth-spurt, every challenge set by their marketer seemed to possess Robert with an unnatural drive. Similar to a thrill seeker, each goal he accomplished only made him reach higher. Although Lainy, Robert's wife, seemed to crave the fruit of his labor as much as her husband craved the success, their marriage had suffered.

Dillon shook his head. He didn't see the growth as a blessing. But trying to slow Robert was like telling a batter on third to walk to home plate. An impossible order.

An ache formed in Dillon's shoulder as it always did whenever he tensed. He rubbed the still tender muscle. Six months didn't seem that long ago. Articles of near-death experiences often spoke of the victims learning to appreciate each day of their lives. Dillon sighed. What was he supposed to appreciate about his brother's choice of nannies?

He heated the tube again then flattened the end with a hammer, careful to leave a vein down the center. The dogwood leaves from the emerald blown glass were already fastened with brass brackets, waiting to be adhered onto the branch.

Dillon glanced back at his drawing. Assured of his plan, he moved to the soldering table and painted a coating of flux over both pieces of copper. The liquid would ensure a strong bond between the copper and solder … much like him and Robert. He stared at the brush in his hand—the same one his dad had started with. A bittersweet memory pinched his heart. Because of Dad, Dillon and Robert were able to make a living doing what they loved.

In his early twenties, Mac Brewington, with his meager savings and a dream, had built a company that now rivaled their giant competitors. If dementia hadn't set in, he'd still be in the shop instead of a nursing home.

"Meow."

Dillon glanced at his feet glad for the distraction. "Hey, Shop Cat." He'd never given the feline a proper name. Then again, he'd never expected it to stick around. On the same day Robert's brake lines were cut, the cat appeared, as curious with the underneath of the car as Dillon had been.

The police report never matched the vandalism with a culprit. Could it have been the same person that shot—Dillon passed off the thought. The day in the woods was a fluke.

***

Emily crossed her legs on the sofa and studied her next move. Jabali was quick, but she'd always been hard to beat at checkers. Playing with the energetic boy the past two weeks had polished her skills with several forgotten childhood games.

Connecting with Rhysa hadn't been as smooth. Rhysa's excitement with the changes in the house mixed with an overdose of distrust kept Emily guessing.

The phone rang and Rhysa answered. "Hi, Mom!" The lilt in her voice was something new to Emily.

"That's nice." A long pause followed as Rhysa listened. "But when are you coming home?"

Another pause. "But you said you'd come back." Rhysa slumped onto the couch beside Emily.

With the girl sitting nearby, Lainy's voice came through the phone. "If you keep whining, I may not want to visit. And I never promised anything."

Silence followed until Lainy spoke again. "Put Robert on the phone."

"Dad's not here.Why would he want to talk to you anyway?" Rhysa's voice rose with each word. "You're the one who left!"

Across from Emily, Jabali fumbled with a checker in his hands. His downcast gaze spoke volumes of disappointment.

The phone startled Emily as it bounced off the cushion beside her. Rhysa stormed from the room wrapped in rage. What was their mother thinking? Granted most marriages had their shares of bumps, but how could she not want to continue a relationship with the children, birthed or adopted?

Reality slapped her in the face. Emily's own mother had left. Funny how the truth of her past hadn't risen to the surface earlier. But unlike many children of divorced homes, Emily and her eldest brother, Ethan, had only to suffer for a couple years. Later, when their dad married Ann, their lives became complete. Ann's genuine love more than made up for the lack of their real mother's. Even after Emily's half siblings were born, nothing changed.

Jabali's sudden loss of interest in the game pulled at Emily's heart. She didn't know everything about the children's backgrounds, but their current pain built a mountain of compassion. "Come on, Jabali. Let's grab your skateboard and go to the park."

The boy's sad eyes sparked. "Okay. I'll tell Rhysa."

Emily straightened the pillows on the couch then waited for them by the garage door, ready to set the house alarm.

Rhysa had her roller blades tucked under her arm. "Do we have to be seen in your car?"

The unexpected insult hurt. What could Rhysa have against Grandpa Luke's old Plymouth? Built in '49, the fat-fendered vehicle was a trophy to Emily. "That's what I'm insured to drive, so be happy we have wheels." The car's antique license worked perfectly for her infrequent stateside visits.

She could have responded with more discipline for the girl's rude behavior, but right now wasn't the time. Rhysa was reacting off her mother's rejection. Emily blinked away sudden tears. Too soft a heart wouldn't help. Rhysa and Jabali needed security. That meant someone to not only love them but to be their strength.

Dillon's face came to mind. Thus far, he hadn't offered his help. But at least the convention ended tomorrow, and their father would return.

Jabali road shotgun while Rhysa slumped in the back seat, trying to hide. Emily dimmed the headlights with her foot. She loved the outdated amenities of old cars like the floor dimmer.

Grandpa had started the restoration of the car while Emily was still a young girl. Offering her help at every stage, he'd allowed her to choose the color. The metallic light green, although pretty, didn't stand out well. Driving with the headlights on insured other drivers would see the vehicle.

At the park, Rhysa took off with the speed of a jet. Did she find them that embarrassing to be seen with or was she only skating off her annoyance with Lainy? Jabali looked back at Emily.

"Ready?"

"Ready." She kept up with him at a fast paced jog, keeping his sister within sight. The park wasn't overly crowded. Still, she never let down her guard.

Lainy came back to mind. Emily wished she could meet the woman to better understand the situation. What drove her away? Jabali had been in the family for the last year and a half, Rhysa, not so long. Had Lainy not been able to deal with the scars of Rhysa's past?

"Rhysa, slow up a bit. You're getting too far ahead."

Although she didn't look back, the girl at least did as asked.

Further up the path, other girls near Rhysa's age slowed as they came closer. Each had a purebred on a leash. Drawing nearer, Emily and Jabali easily overheard them.

"Hey, looky there, it's the Russian Sasquatch." Their mocking cackles increased in volume.

Jabali skid his skateboard to a stop. Blocking their path, he demanded, "Apologize to my sister, or I'll put a curse on you!"

Shocked expressions stared at Jabali then expanded into smiles as one girl blurted, "Oh, we're so scared."

Emily looked toward Rhysa whose pain-filled eyes touched on her brother, but narrowed and broke contact when they met Emily's.

Emily tapped Jabali's arm as the girls passed. "Let's go."

For all the hurt Lainy put the children through, they certainly didn't need additional trouble from their peers. No wonder Robert hadn't wanted Rhysa to endure summer school.

Humiliation and shame were now added elements to the difficult equation Emily had agreed to. Her situation would be easier if there was another adult she could share with. But Maurita spoke very little English and Dillon was as helpful as roller blades without wheels.

They continued on the path although it was clear the zeal for the park had vanished. What should she have done? Thinking over the ugly scene, Emily wished she'd have handled it better. Shocked by the unexpected verbal attack, followed by Jabali's remark, what could she have done?

At the car, Rhysa climbed in without removing her skates, only to slink down in the seat. Not a word. No show of emotion.

Emily never had to deal with the pressure to fit in. Homeschool shielded her from so many ugly realities. Still, like Rhysa, her size often bothered her, too. A part of Emily accredited it to her single state. Men wanted Barbie dolls—at least that's what the media suggested. She glanced at the two broken children. This wasn't about her.

"God, I realize why I'm here. It's not for me as much as for these children. Give me the wisdom to steer them closer to you. Guide me in growing Jabali's faith so that he never feels the need to fall back on superstitions from his homeland. Let Your belt of truth wrap around him as a protection from the enemy's cunning deceit.

"And Rhysa," her heart squeezed with pain, *"this child, dear Lord, is filled with misery. She feels abandoned and rejected. Guide me in proving to her she is lovely, not only in Your sight but in mine as well. Open both of the children's hearts to receive Your love and mine."*

Emily slid in next to Jabali and turned the key.

"Ah-h-h!" A large black spider sat on the dashboard, unmoving.

Jabali clapped his hands. "Good! This works very good. My spider kept your car safe."

"What?" Only after the boy removed it to the floor did Emily realize it wasn't real. "Ja—"

Laughter from the back seat erupted from Rhysa. "I saw your eyes in the mirror." Rhysa snorted, "They were huge!"

Jabali's white toothed grin joined Rhysa's.

"Very funny, guys, so the joke's on me." Emily shook her head. Although she didn't support Jabali's superstitions, she welcomed the lightened atmosphere.

Emily had planned on stopping for ice cream, but under the circumstances it might only bring the girls' comment from the park back to the surface. "How would you two like to get a movie for tonight?"

"Yeah, the new Monsters movie!" Jabali looked back at his sister.

Rhysa nodded. "That's good for me."

"As long as there aren't any spiders in it, I'm okay." Emily teased, knowing the cartoon's light-hearted humor would be good for them.

Thank You, Lord, for giving this evening another chance.

After stopping at a Red Box, they pulled into the lane leading home. Jabali strained his head to see around to the shop. "Aw, I was hoping Uncle Dillon would watch it with us."

"You can ask him."

"No. His truck's gone."

Emily was sorry for the boy's disappointment. Part of her shared the feeling. It would have been fun to see how the artistic recluse reacted to a humorous film. Did he have a sense of humor?

Inside the garage, the children grabbed their park gear and were out before she had time to gather the movie and her purse.

Rhysa leaned away from the open door leading into the house. Her voice soft and timid, "I thought you set the alarm?"

"I did.

Chapter Three

Reason and fear warred inside Emily. Perhaps the cook had forgotten to lock the door on her way out. Or maybe Dillon needed something from the garage before he left. Her excuses did little to quiet the tiny bells of alarm ringing inside her head.

The kitchen was clean and empty. The smell of grilled meat and cilantro stirred the rumblings in Emily's stomach. She'd become accustomed to the cook's habits. Maurita arrived in the morning and left in the late afternoon but not before leaving a prepared dinner in the oven with the timer set to cook or warm.

"Maybe Maurita left the door unlocked?" Emily spoke to Rhysa and Jabali as they trailed close behind.

Rhysa shook her head. "She uses the front door. Even if she forgot to set the alarm, this door should have been locked."

Emily pointed toward the wall phone. "Call your uncle while I search the house." A marble rolling pin sat cradled in its wooden holder on the kitchen island. Emily crowded the counter on her way out, discreetly claiming her defense.

The large house grew with the thought of an intruder. Emily forced herself to breathe steadily. Her heart knew with faith she had no reason to fear. But her head begged to differ.

She stood in the entrance of the sitting room examining potential hiding places before taking a closer look. An overstuffed chair in the corner posed the only threat. Emily crept around the sofa and neared the hearth. With the rolling pin raised to swing, she jumped onto the cushioned seat and searched between the chair and wall—nothing.

Emily's heartbeat quickened, shaming her with obvious fear. The dread of someone jumping out unexpectedly likened itself to hide and seek. The childhood game hadn't been one of her favorites then and it certainly wasn't now.

She crept toward the office then paused beside the door. Should she fling it open and rush inside? Or would turning the knob slowly be more advantageous? Wanting it all to be over, she chose the former.

Her hand tightened around the brass then slipped, scraping her knuckles against the wooden frame. Locked. *That's a good sign, right?* Emily took a deep breath. Where to look next?

Even before she turned, the weight of an ominous cloud settled around her. The wide staircase morphed into a giant mouth, ready to snap closed as soon as her feet touched the ivory colored teeth. She fought off a shiver. "Yea, though I walk through the valley of the shadow of death, I will fear no evil: for thou art with me; thy rod and thy staff they comfort me."

The twenty-third Psalms played as a mantra inside her head. Emily remembered standing in front of their small congregation with other children from their booster choir. Without any fear to hold her back, she'd repeated the whole chapter with confidence. Where was her confidence now?

The hall off the sitting room loomed with playful shadows. Playful felt safer than ominous. She'd save the upstairs for last. But the evening sun attested time had slipped by. Unease irritated the base of Emily's neck. It would soon be dark and switching on the lights would only give her away.

To whom? Perhaps no one had entered and all of this was for nothing. Unfortunately there was only one way to find out.

Emily tiptoed down the hall leading to the master bedroom. A room she had no need to enter before. The door opened on silent hinges and butted against the wall. *Okay, no one hiding behind it.* A garden tub with splendid pillars was in the corner accentuated by potted palm trees and large paintings of the beach. On the opposite side of the room, covered in regal gold and bronze bedding sat a king size bed.

Emily cringed. *Oh, I don't want to have to look under that.* She swallowed past the lump in her throat and forced wooden legs to move. The plush carpeting softened her steps. With the rolling pin held tight in her grip, she bent at the knees. Her mouth formed a tight line. *It's now or never.* She reached for the bed skirt and flipped it back.

Boxes.

A deep breath filled her lungs. Bending forward, she rested her head against the floor. *This is probably all for nothing and I'm just being silly.*

The master bath was next. Darkened by the lack of windows, Emily flipped the light-switch. This was one area it would be foolish to approach in the dark.

The fluorescent bulbs flickered as the fixture began to hum. Not the perfect time to wear out.

Though dim, the lighting provided enough to see by. As if the garden tub wasn't enough, the room was complete with a shower for two and a long double sink. And ... a walk-in closet.

"Being alone stinks." Emily mumbled beneath her breath. If she were married, she'd have a husband to depend on. Someone to come to her aid—a protector. But God had chosen a different route for her life.

Guilt pricked her conscious. *Okay, I'm not alone. God is with me. And He's all the power I need.* Her back straightened with determination as she lifted the rolling pin. *Just swing with me, God.* The closet door opened wide. Light trickled forward from the bathroom, creating dark, creepy forms along the wall.

She settled a timid foot into the room, then another while feeling for a light switch along the wall. Like a turtle stretching its neck, Emily craned to see around the door.

"Emily!"

She screamed and spun around, bringing the rolling pin crashing down.

"A-h-h!" Dillon stumbled backward, rattling the shower door.

Her mouth dropped open—She'd struck her employer's brother.

"Oops." Emily hadn't expected Dillon so soon. He must've driven home as soon as the kids called him. She eased the offending object behind her back and rocked on her heels. "I thought you were the intruder."

He grimaced and rubbed his shoulder. "Why would the intruder use your name?"

She glanced to the side then tapped a finger against her bottom lip. "Um … I guess he wouldn't."

Dillon reached for her weapon. "This should stay in the kitchen, which is where I'm taking you."

He touched her back to propel her forward, but pulled her to a stop at the doorway to the hall. "Where have you searched?"

Despite their circumstances, the interesting tingle left by his fingers couldn't be denied. She looked up, hoping to get a better look at his eyes to satisfy her curiosity from before. The dim lighting still hid them from view. "Everywhere but upstairs."

"Saved the best for last, huh?" A semblance of a smile teased the corner of his mouth before he diverted his attention.

Dillon checked the hall then stepped out first. After he escorted her to the kitchen to join his niece and nephew, he replaced the rolling pin.

Emily pointed toward the counter. "Don't you want that?"

He smirked and patted a bicep. "I don't need it."

Did their uncle have a sense of humor after all?

Jabali's hand slipped into hers. She glanced toward him and noted Rhysa had also crowded close. She squeezed Jabali's hand and gave Rhysa a smile of encouragement. A fear of the unknown etched worry lines across Rhysa's forehead.

They needed a distraction. Emily cleared her throat and motioned toward the oven. "Have you checked what Maurita left us for dinner?"

Rhysa blinked in surprise and then did as suggested. "Grilled chicken. And I bet mango salsa's in the fridge."

Jabali sprung forward. "I'll check!"

Thank you for the distraction, Lord, but please keep Dillon safe. The children had enough upsets in their lives. Why had this one been allowed? Surely God wouldn't let anything happen to their uncle, he was the only steady security they had. She peeked toward the stairs before setting out the flatware.

***

The last room was Jabali's, and still Dillon hadn't found anything suggesting a prowler.

"Robert." Dillon stood in front of the baseball collection with his cell phone and commanded his brother's attention. The possibility that someone had broken into the house had created a bigger stir in him than Dillon would've expected. He cradled the phone with one hand as the other massaged his shoulder. Emily's swing could rival a Cardinal batter. "I searched the house, nobody's here. It was probably just a fluke."

"Where are the kids?" Worry deepened his brother's voice.

"With Emily. I think they're getting dinner on the table." He leaned out of the room and listened past the hallway. "She sure has a knack with them."

Robert sighed through the phone. A moment passed before he spoke again. "Things have been weird here, too."

Now it was Dillon's turn to be surprised. His spine stiffened preparing for bad news.

"I was certain of being followed last week. But it seems this week's schedule threw them off."

"What are you saying? Someone knew you'd be at the convention, or—"

"I'll ... I'll talk to you about it tomorrow. I should be home by the afternoon. Just keep a close eye on everyone."

The room darkened as apprehension roared in the pit of Dillon's stomach. His got-it-together brother was struggling. Who was behind this? And better yet, why? With a sudden urgency, Dillon headed toward the stairs.

Dillon slowed to as he neared the kitchen. Voices floated through the air in assurance no harm had come to them while he was gone.

Emily met his gaze from across the informal table. "Everything check out okay?"

Jabali and Rhysa's attentive silence revealed they too were waiting for his answer.

"Empty as a to—" He stopped himself. Not the expression needed in this situation. "Safe and sound. The way I expected to find it."

Though it seemed they could breathe easier, he wasn't certain of their security.

After dinner, Dillon piled his plate on the counter. He was anxious to return to the cottage and check for intruders while waiting to hear from Robert.

"Uncle Dillon. Now that you're home, you can watch a movie with us!" Jabali's bright, expressive face was hard to refuse. But other things took priority.

"Jabali, I—"

"I'm sure he'd love to. After all, he's probably lonely being by himself all the time."

Dillon judged her tight smile and realized she'd be hard to beat in an argument. Nothing new there. Robert was the same way. "Fine. Why don't you get it started while Rhysa pops corn? I'll be right back."

He slid out of what was beginning to feel like a crowded room and crossed the lawn. Emily's wide-eyed expression interrupted his concentration and drew a smile to his lips. He was supposed to be keeping an eye out for intruders, not grinning over being attacked. He rotated his shoulder and readjusted his thoughts. The cottage and shop were dark, just as he'd left them. But were they as empty as they appeared?

Dillon slowed as he neared the custom stained-glass door. The knob jiggled. Still locked. If it hadn't been for his brother's attack, Dillon might have passed off Emily's concern. But the flukes, as he had called the bizarre events of the year, were adding up.

The small efficiency was clean of intruders but not his piles of drawings. His leg brushed against a stack on the side table, sending papers fluttering to the floor. Ignoring them, he relocked the door.

Moments later he met Emily at the end of the path back to the house. Her arms crossed over her chest. Had he done something wrong?

"Sorry if I seemed demanding." She gestured toward the kitchen with her head. "But the kids need your presence and …" She rocked back on her heels again. "It looked like you were keeping something from them. What did you find?"

So he hadn't done anything wrong. A strange feeling tensed Dillon's muscles. He didn't want the kids' nanny to have anything to fear. "Nothing. Safe and sound, just like I said."

His phone chose that time to ring. He reached into his shirt pocket. "Start the movie. I'll be just a minute."

She went back inside. An odd feeling lingered after her departure. But time didn't allow for consideration.

Dillon answered the phone. "Robert?"

"Sleep light." His brother sighed into the receiver. "While I was out, someone took the liberty of searching my room."

Dillon reached for the door, no longer content to be apart from the family. Robert's news meant whoever had tailed him last week, had caught up. "Change your schedule, fly home tonight."

"Already tried and failed. But I'll hang out at the airport. I might get a shot at a stand-by ticket. If nothing else, it's at least public."

***

Dillon settled into the easy chair across from the sofa. The children's thoughtfulness to reserve the seat for him was touching, but since taking Robert's calls he would've preferred the floor. Anxiety coiled in his muscles, making him ready to spring like a cat.

He leaned back and tried to relax. Although he'd rather be forming a plan, the children needed the security of his presence. And if Dillon didn't know better, their nanny did too.

Despite the need for caution, the movie pulled him in. Whether the scenes were actually humorous enough to laugh, it was impossible not to be affected by the other occupants in the room.

Jabali, the most comedic one of them all, kept tossing his head back with his mouth split in a wide grin. Even Rhysa was tickled over several scenes. The light of the television flickered off her features, exposing dimples he rarely saw. How long had it been since he'd seen her happy? He wished it would last.

Did Emily know Rhysa's history? The years she'd spent in an Ukranian orphanage or of her birth mother's occupation? Daughter of a prostitute, Rhysa had witnessed more than most people did in a lifetime, let alone in six years. Emotional scars were often as damaging as physical ones. No wonder she rarely smiled and suffered sudden outbursts of anger.

Some might say Rhysa was the reason Lainy left, but Dillon knew better. Money had changed her from someone compassionate enough to want to help children to a woman focused on her needs alone.

And Robert thought him senseless to have given up on finding Mrs. Right. If his brother's marriage was anything to go by, Dillon had made the right decision.

Emily erupted with laughter. Her laugh drew attention and the others shared in her joy. He turned enough to view her in his peripheral vision without being noticeable.

There was nothing pretentious about the woman. Completely relaxed and at ease with who she was. She chuckled again and glanced his direction. Now he knew what his brother thought he was missing. Shared moments like these, surrounded by family.

He also understood the concern Robert expressed tonight. Until they knew who was responsible for the attempts and why, no one was safe.

***

"So how'd the past two weeks go?" Robert poured Raisin Bran into his bowl.

The sun had yet to rise and Emily was already up. She leaned against the kitchen island with a cup of coffee and stifled a yawn. Her employer had arrived home earlier than expected, surprising her by coming through the garage door as she entered the kitchen. "That depends. Do you want a pat answer or an honest one?"

"Honest, of course." He cringed.

From the look of his unshaven face and shadowed eyes, Emily preferred to give a pat description, but he'd never be satisfied. "You left me with two insecure orphans who feel orphaned all over again, one of which definitely resents my presence, a maid who speaks very little English, and a brother who lacks most social skills."

Emily pulled a chair back from the table and sat at the opposite end from Robert. She gave a good-hearted smile and joked, "My optimism was only held in check by your quick return."

"Hmm." Robert cupped his chin in his hand. "I thought you said you spoke Spanish?"

"I did, years ago. But never at Maurita's speed. I'm not complaining about her, we get along great. It's just with your brother being such a recluse, it would be nice to have another adult to talk to, especially concerning the children."

A long sigh resulted from the mention of his brother. Robert glanced toward the door. "Don't let his aloof behavior discourage you. He's always been shy around new people."

"Why do I get the feeling he tries to keep everyone new?"

A chuckle rumbled from Robert's throat. "Don't let him run you off either. You're exactly what this family needs. Isn't there a verse you should be drawing from right now?"

Emily gave a sheepish shrug. "Yes, several. And what about you? You're life isn't exactly peachy from what I gather. What verses give you strength?"

"Second Corinthians twelve, verses nine and ten."

She knew the familiar passage. *And he said unto me, My grace is sufficient for thee; for my strength is made perfect in weakness. Most gladly therefore will I rather glory in my infirmities that the power of Christ may rest upon me. Therefore I take pleasure in infirmities, in reproaches, in necessities, in persecutions, in distresses for Christ's sake: for when I am weak, then am I strong.*

Robert rose from the table. "Time to start the day. Remember you have off tomorrow, then I'm gone again on Monday."

Her thoughts collided before she could give thought to her Sunday off. Concern tightened her chest. "You're leaving again already?"

"Yes, but don't worry. I'll talk to the kids about their behavior."

Emily's heart sank. Did he not listen? The children needed him. And what about his brother? Was she completely on her own?

Chapter Four

Several weeks later ...

Dillon returned to the cul-de-sac with his truck loaded with material for work and his usual Friday morning treat of doughnuts. He'd started the ritual before school let out for the summer and now the kids had come to expect it. Emily waved as she passed him in her ancient set of wheels. Robert had mentioned sending her on a few errands today. Fearless, she pulled onto the road alive with early morning commuters. Dillon watched the car fade from view.

"God, keep her safe in that thing." Not that he didn't have an appreciation for antique vehicles, but Emily's Plymouth wasn't in pristine condition. He repeated the prayer each time she climbed behind the giant steering wheel.

His foot eased off the brake as he continued home. The smooth stone siding of his cottage reflected that of the main house. Robert's good taste not only complimented the community but also boasted of his success. His leadership skills went beyond growing the business and reached those who helped it survive, the employees. The lack of employee turnover proved their satisfaction.

Then why would anyone hold a vendetta against Robert? His brother might have moved past the concern, but the scar in Dillon's shoulder served as a constant reminder ... and threat.

As he pulled to the back of the shop to unload, he saw Jabali pitch a ball to his dad. He had a good arm, thanks to the time Robert spent with him last summer—before the business took off.

Robert turned and flicked his wrist to throw the ball, but not to Jabali. "Good catch, Rhysa."

Rhysa was playing ball?

Dillon stepped from the cab and studied the triangle made by father, son, and daughter—a picturesque scene. For the moment, the children were happy and content. But it wouldn't last. In less than two days Robert would leave again. Didn't he realize how much the kids missed his presence?

If Lainy would step in, the transition wouldn't be as hard on the children, but until she figured out if she wanted a divorce or not, she'd chosen to distance herself. Unfortunately, nothing Dillon or their nanny did could make up for their parents' absence. And similar to the sufferings of divorce, the children's internal needs were overlooked as mom and dad struggled to make sense of their own breaking hearts.

Time slipped by as Dillon organized the new material then began work on another project. This one a lamp to compliment a hanging ceiling fixture.

He dropped a pipe and didn't hear Robert enter as the long cylinder clanged against the concrete floor.

"Hey, stranger."

Dillon turned at the sound of his brother's voice. He positioned the copper on its base as he spoke. "You picked a good day for being outside."

"Yeah." Robert tossed the ball into his mitt. "I've been missing the kids."

"They love it when you're home." Did Dillon venture further and speak his mind? He took the chance. "You could always make more time for them Slowing down doesn't mean we'll lose business." He massaged his tense shoulder. Several weeks had passed since the intrusion in his brother's motel room. The lack of "events" seemed to fuel Robert's drive as he continued to pile on more.

Dillon tightened the pole on its base with a wrench. "Just strengthen where we're at."

"The growth isn't just because I enjoy that part of the business." Robert paced the length of the worktable in front of Dillon. "Lainy didn't have money growing up. I'm doing this for her."

As if the air had been sucked from the room, Dillon gasped. "What? She's not even acting as your wife—"

"You don't know everything there is to know. Becoming an instant mom wasn't as easy as Lainy thought it would be. She did fine with Jabali, but Rhysa's different. When we hosted her, she seemed a lot more subdued. Her problems didn't show up until after the adoption."

Dillon inwardly moaned. How could his brother be so blind? Didn't he see that Rhysa wasn't the main problem, but that the additional money had changed Lainy? "This isn't all about Rhysa's temper. Lainy's changed—a lot. I don't know how you can still love her."

"By loving God more."

Robert's reply weakened Dillon's argument.

"I vowed to be her husband through better or worse." Robert let out a lengthy sigh. "This is worse.

But until God releases me from my duties, I'm going to take care of her."

Dillon shook his head, unable to wrap his mind around what his brother said. "What if she's unfaithful? The Bible gives you room—"

Robert's hand shot up to warn him. Dillon dropped the subject and stared at the metal on the worktable, tempted to pound his frustrations into the near finished project. But it would solve nothing. Neither would talking to his heart-sick brother.

***

"Meow."

Dillon's gaze followed Shop Cat's to the window. He shoved his loupes lenses on top his head. Emily strolled down the path, stopped to remove dead flower bulbs from an iris bed then resumed her way to the shop. Dillon's heart picked up its pace.

Over a month had passed since Emily accepted the nanny position and he still didn't know much about her except she'd be gone come fall.

And that she had a laugh that could pull a smile from anyone.

Not to mention a great smile.

A light tap sounded on the stained glass. Emily entered. "Sorry to bother you, but the kids want to know if you'll join us for dinner. They made it themselves."

A knit headband held Emily's hair away from her face allowing him full view of her features. Soft skin and vivid eyes brought extra warmth to the room.

Her lips pulled in a smile. "What are you looking at?"

Dillon smiled, unwilling to drop his gaze. "I like your hair. Looks good that way."

Emily blushed but didn't drop her chin. Yet another admirable quality. She could accept a compliment.

"Thank you, but are you coming?"

"Sure, I'll be there after I clean up." He watched her go, glad for the invitation. He'd tried to keep his distance, but in truth, she intrigued him. Ever since her first trip home a sad, small cloud seemed to hover over her. Her eyes weren't as bright nor her smile as wide. Was she reluctant to leave the states again? Did it matter to Dillon?

Dinner turned out to be an assortment of exotic dishes, including something from everyone's homeland. Maurita had agreed to stay and enjoy the fruit of their labors. Pushing a platter of something wrapped in corn tortillas, she urged Dillon to scoop more onto his plate.

"What are they?" Suspicion cautioned his appetite. "*Cuales son estos?*" He repeated the question in Spanish and raised a questioning brow toward his brother.

"Very good!" Maurita smiled and nodded to the rest of the family, their smiles growing with hers.

Dillon glanced over the counter and spotted a jar of hot sauce and peppers. No doubt they planned to surprise him. Little did they know the tolerance of his palette. He picked up the rolled entrée and shoved it in his mouth. A light fire hit the back of his throat. Dillon smiled around the food and gave a mock bow. He turned to Robert. "Are you too soft?"

Giggles sounded from around the table.

He chewed the last of his bite and reached for another roll. Then the aftermath hit. Flames leapt from the back of his throat to the roof of his mouth. Even his teeth seemed to cringe in pain. Dillon fumbled for his glass. Water toppled over the rim and ran down his chin as he slurped.

"Good?" Maurita's eyes sought for approval.

Seriously? How could anyone enjoy swallowing a torch?

Emily had left the table and returned with a glass of milk. Dillon downed the cure before settling back in his chair. "A little hot, Maurita." His voice sounded as hoarse as a kid who'd just smoked a grape vine on a dare.

She smiled and nodded. "I take these home to my *mi esposo*."

"If your husband can eat them, he's more of a man than me. And to think, I thought we were friends." He tossed a wink toward Emily and wiggled the empty milk glass. "I guess I found my new best friend."

A blush captured her for the second time this evening. He was on a roll.

Their cook grinned and shoved a different plate forward. "You try these. Not so hot."

Dillon waved his hand and passed them toward his brother. "Maybe later. First I'll try the other dishes." His throat still raw, he coughed out the last of his sentence.

After dinner, Dillon stood beside his brother's car.

Robert loaded his suit case into the trunk. "I only have four hours of driving time tonight. I'll leave the motel for the morning meeting tomorrow and then be home for dinner."

"Unless something else is scheduled." Dillon wanted to make certain Robert's careless calendar was known by all. "The kids would do better if you stuck to a tighter schedule."

Robert rubbed the top of the car as if checking the paint, when in reality he was stalling for an excuse.

"Drive safe and God speed." Dillon relieved him of the awkward moment. Perhaps he'd want to run, too, if home stood as a constant reminder of what he didn't have.

"Thanks. I will." Robert climbed behind the wheel and was gone again.

Dillon slipped through the back door of the garage and walked toward the cottage. Inside, he stared at the mess. What if Emily saw this? The urge to clean hit him by surprise. Her opinion shouldn't matter, but it did. The memory of her blush brought a smile to his lips. He enjoyed teasing her. Maybe too much.

He needed a good slap.

Don't leave your heart where it isn't wanted. Hadn't experience taught him as much?

Dillon grabbed the dishes scattered in the living room and loaded the washer. No longer cleaning for anyone's opinion, frustration overtook the job. Once the sinks were clean and the vacuum ran in each room, he finally stopped and plopped into his easy chair.

How could he get her to stay? The question surprised him, but was worth considering. If Emily felt needed here more than overseas it might persuade her not to leave. Dillon couldn't let her know it was for his sake, but if the kids became too attached … what type of man was he? God would direct Emily where she was needed and all he could do was … what? Stand by and watch?

He ran a hand through his hair then let his arm fall to the side. His hand whacked against a hasty stack of papers littering the end table. Left untouched since the night he'd searched for an intruder, Dillon picked up the pile and knocked the sides down until the corners came together.

He cocked his head and blinked, then brought the drawing closer to the lamplight.

Smeared on top—a shoe print.

Dillon shot from his chair. He glanced around the room. Who had been here and why? A search of the closets, the only places he hadn't cleaned, revealed nothing.

Dillon ground his teeth and slammed his fist on the end table. The paper floated to the side. The shoe print was too small to be a man's. But the kids had been watching a movie the night he'd searched. It couldn't have been them.

Who had a vendetta against Robert, had keys to the buildings—his phone rang from where he'd left it in the living room.

The main house. He rubbed his temple and put the phone to his ear.

"Dillon, I need you." Emily's voice came out in a rush. "We have an intruder."

Deafening silence robbed his thoughts, before Dillon raced out the door and across the yard. He'd been in the house tonight. So had Robert. How did someone sneak in?

He slipped inside the back door and crept through the kitchen. His heartbeat mimicked a set of drums inside his head. Toward the front room came two female voices.

"Stay where you are."

"You're going to be sorry. You don't have any right to threaten me!"

He slowed to a stop. Not far from the steps, exposed by the outdoor lighting shining through the window, stood Emily, poised with the heavy base of a lamp. A twinge shot through his shoulder, reminding him of her strength. Strength he was certain the intruder wouldn't want to encounter.

He flipped the light switch.

Emily answered, "She cut the power."

"Don't be stupid. I only flipped the main breaker."

That voice. Dillon blinked through the darkness. The silky, smooth tone belonged to someone who knew where to find the main breaker. She had access to the buildings ...

"Lainy?"

Silence stretched until his sister-in-law finally chose to speak. "That's right. Now that you've finally caught on, you can flip the breaker in the garage."

From beside the window, Emily motioned toward him. "Go ahead. She's not going anywhere."

Dillon had to smile. Lainy's voice carried a cultured, false commodity. Emily's was blunt and brave.

Within moments, he returned to find both women seated across from each other. Emily sat with the lamp near enough to reach.

Dillon leaned against the wall to better judge Lainy's expression. He crossed his arms over his chest. "You can start explaining yourself anytime."

Clad in black, Robert's wife gave a delicate shrug. "I certainly don't owe an explanation. This is still my house." She stretched an arm over the cushion, petting the fabric as if it were a cat.

Irritation built in Dillon's gut. What was the self-indulgent woman up to? Though it'd been years since he'd held a good opinion of Lainy, to think she'd stoop to murder had never seemed a possibility. Until now. Still, he clenched his jaw shut to keep from saying too much. He needed her relaxed and loose lipped.

"You're right, it is your house. However, when one feels the need to dress in black and sneak in unannounced ..."

"Fine. Have it your way," she uncrossed her legs then crossed them again, tapping her foot in the air. "Robert hasn't sent my rent check and he hasn't answered my calls."

She pinned her eyes on Emily. "I thought there might have been a reason."

Emily's spine straightened as her eyes darted toward Dillon.

He jumped to her defense. "Emily is our temporary nanny. If that bothers you, I suggest you fulfill your role as mother to Rhsya and Jabali."

Indignation colored Lainy's cheeks. She leapt to her feet and turned toward Dillon. Her words hissed out in a tightly controlled anger. "Just write me a check."

Her statements confused him. The only reason she'd need a check is if she and Robert didn't share an account.

Dillon moved toward the kitchen knowing Lainy would follow. He didn't want her waking the children. "I don't know what your situation is, Lainy, but I don't have access to Robert's account. However," he motioned around the room, "rent here is free."

He didn't want her back, not like this, but she was Robert's wife, the children's adopted mother. For them, he would encourage her.

Her fists tightened at her sides. "Just tell your brother to pay my rent." She turned and stormed out the back door.

Dillon joined Emily at the front window. Lainy crawled into a car parked a few houses down. The vehicle was a different model than Robert had purchased for her. Perhaps she'd traded it in.

"That stirs up some questions." Emily flipped her hair over her shoulder and strolled toward the kitchen.

Dillon stared after her a moment before following. Dressed in cotton sleepwear, Emily's pinstriped, baseball themed short and shirt pajamas, added to her appealing nature. There was something about the nanny that set her apart. Too bad she'd leave in the fall.

In the kitchen, he opened the cupboard. "I can make a mean cup of hot cocoa. You interested, number one?" Dillon referred to the number on her shirt.

"Sure. And if I'm up all night I'll plot ways to keep prowlers out of the house." Emily joined him by the counter, bringing with her a fruity floral scent. No wonder he'd stayed immersed in his work, the woman had an innocent way of wreaking havoc on his senses.

"And what would your first suggestion be for tightening our security?" He tried to wrap his mind around anything but her and opened two packets of instant hot chocolate mix. The short-cut he took would be made up for once he added whipped topping and cinnamon. He whipped the mix and milk together then passed the cups to Emily to heat in the microwave.

"Well, this may not be enough, but I thought a moat filled with alligators might be a good deterrent." Emily fought to keep her mouth in a serious line. A small dimple formed to the side before a smile split across her lightly freckled face.

No way could he focus on other things now.

"I doubt that's needed. I saw the way you wield a lamp. And I'm still feeling the rolling pin."

Emily spun around from removing the cups from the microwave. "Oh, is it bruised?" The milk sloshed over the rim as Dillon moved to accept his cup. The hot chocolate splashed onto his chest.

"Whoa!" Dillon bent over and tugged the steaming shirt away from his skin.

"Uh oh." Emily set the cups on the counter in a rush then yanked the material from his back, drawing it over his head. "Here, take it off."

With his arms caught in his shirt and not wanting to have the hot material against his face, Dillon's only choice was to comply. He twisted the rest of the way out and took the stained shirt to the sink. Between chokes of laughter, Dillon spoke over the running water. "You sure do react fast."

Chocolate milk ran down the sink in a small river. As he reached for the soap, her fingers grazed across the back of his shoulder and trailed to his arm. Fuzzy warmth filled his chest. He hadn't given thought to acting on the attraction he felt—he'd hardly even accepted it. Did Emily know what she was doing? He turned to meet her lips.

Her furrowed forehead was all that faced him. Her hand moved to the front of his collarbone. "How did you get this?"

Dillon cleared his throat. Glad his misguided thoughts hadn't been exposed. "I was in an accident."

Liquid blue eyes looked up to meet his. A silence hung in the air as she searched for answers to unspoken questions. "Hazel eyes."

Her gaze fell back to his shoulder. "You were shot."

Was he slow tonight or was she not making any sense? How did his color of eyes tell what his scar was from?

She whispered, "While hunting. But you had a beard then."

Everything in the room seemed to disappear. He was alone in the woods again and cold. Very cold. "How do you know that?" Even as he asked the question, a part of him knew. Her voice. He could hear it now. Telling him she would come back. Dillon placed his hand over hers, pressing her skin against the healed wound.

A timid smile played on her lips. Her eyes fluttered to hold back tears. "I didn't know if you'd made it." She took in a deep breath ending with a whispered sigh, "I've always wondered."

Dillon turned off the water and touched her face. "So it's you I have to thank."

A charge shot from her skin through his hand. The air thinned while the room around them dimmed. Awareness heightened Dillon's senses. Were they ready for this? He stepped back before he did something crazy. Her eyes moved back to the scar. Some primitive desire wished she'd touch him again.

A tiny gasp sounded. "Were you shot twice?"

Dillon rubbed a hand over the spot and nodded. What could he say? Hey, stop staring and get me a shirt? He turned. Robert wouldn't mind his borrowing one.

"Then it wasn't an accident."

He rubbed his temple. The same thought had tempted him on several occasions. "I'll get a shirt. Then we'll talk."

Boy, it was a good thing they were usually hands off. He'd stepped away knowing if he didn't Emily would've been wrapped in his arms. He drew a deep breath. She was leaving in four months. No. Now it was less than three. He didn't want what every other guy he knew seemed to deal with. Fleeing women.

Dad's situation was different. Mom had died. Still, her death left a gaping emptiness in Dad, creating a welcome mat for dementia.

He flipped the light in Robert's room. Had Lainy searched here as well? He paused by the side table. Robert had their wedding picture displayed by his clock.

Lainy's appearance hadn't always been so refined. Her now sleek highlighted hair had once been dry and brittle. Even her makeup had changed from what Dillon considered normal to cosmopolitan. Funny how social status played a significant role in some people and not in others.

Robert and Dillon's parents had been well off but never wore their money for show. They looked for bargains at thrift stores and still supported the local grocer rather than a big chain. The biggest change he'd seen in them when the business had grown was how much they were able to give. Helping out a fellow neighbor or church member who'd fallen on bad times came as natural as paying their tithe. Too bad Mom had already passed when Lainy came into the family. If given the opportunity, Lainy might have turned out differently.

Dillon returned and found his shirt washed and drying on the sink. Emily sat at the table with pen and paper in hand.

"I'm a goal setter and a planner." Her shining gaze darted to his healed shoulder and back. She blinked against the building moisture. Had learning he was alive meant that much to her?

Emily continued. "My skill set revolves around my organizing skills, so let's put it to work."

Dillon settled in the adjacent chair, still mesmerized that fate would bring them together again. He joined in her attempt to move along in conversation. It was probably for the best. "What do you have started?"

Emily turned the paper around for him to see. "Columns."

She wasn't kidding. Vertical lines separated two empty columns, save for their titles. Dillon found himself smiling again, something he hadn't done very much of before she arrived

"I hope you get paid well for your talent."

A snicker slipped from her coral lips. They were perfectly formed, not too thin, not too full. Dillon cleared his throat and directed his attention back to the sheet. "How—why do you have attempts and bad guys written down?"

"I heard you on the phone." She tapped the pen between her fingers. "The night the alarm wasn't set. I'd started to step back outside ... I didn't stay and listen, but I heard you repeat that Robert's room had been searched."

Dillon absorbed the information. She'd known there was more to be concerned about. Yet she didn't question, and thankfully, hadn't packed and left. "And now I guess I'm supposed to fill in?"

"Yes, but I'll help with the first one." She reclaimed the sheet and penned, *shooting,* beneath the attempts column.

"We don't know for sure it wasn't an accident."

"Why were you out there?" Her eyes narrowed. "You don't seem like the hunter-type of guy."

He rubbed his temple. "No, I'm not. But we've all grown used to having venison in the freezer thanks to Robert. This was his trip, but he couldn't go for some reason. I think it had to do with the kids. One of them was sick or something."

"Hmm. So Robert was supposed to be the hunter." She pulled a knee up to her chest and tapped the pen against her lip. "Who knew about this planned trip?"

"Most people, I guess. It's no secret he likes hunting in that part of the state. Not too many other hunters to contend with."

An hour of discussion later, Dillon said good night. The usual comfort of home had been replaced. He felt uneasy leaving the house, but at least he'd been able to call the security company and change the code.

Coyotes yowled. They were closer than usual. Shop Cat bounded up the trail. Reaching his paws high on Dillon's leg, he gave a pitiful meow. Dillon reached for the cat. "I know what you want."

Once inside the house, Dillon slipped the cat inside the carrier. Though not allowed free run of the cottage, the feline seemed to appreciate the shared hospitality.

He supported his weight against the door and removed his shoes. A framed photograph struck him as odd. Shoved from its usual spot on top the bookcase, it now rested against the wall. Judging from the small shoe print, Lainy had searched his cottage more thoroughly than he would've expected. What was she looking for—a checkbook?

Dillon unfolded the sheet of paper containing the ideas Emily had written. The only person he could think of that might want Robert gone was Lainy. But why would she if she couldn't even write a check from their account? He glanced at the clock. Like it or not, he was calling Robert.

Chapter Five

Emily rolled to the side of her bed and stood. Maybe she was hungry. She filled a glass of milk downstairs and carried it back to her room. She paced across the carpet and as she emptied the small glass. With all the thoughts and emotions swirling in her head, milk wasn't the answer to her restlessness. She grabbed her prayer journal. God was her favorite pen pal. Through pen and paper she could write what she lacked the courage to say out loud.

Should she start with Lainy? The children? Robert's safety? Even though they all needed prayer, another would intrude on their time if she didn't take care of him first. Dillon.

A heavy sigh relaxed her shoulders. Amazed that Dillon was alive, it was equally amazing that God would direct her right to him. What did the Master Planner have up His sleeve? He'd undoubtedly called her to missions as was proven with each assignment. Confused, she addressed her questions in ink.

Leaning back in the chair, she knew the subject of missions wasn't the issue. Instead, the real issue was the sensational thrill from connecting with Dillon. Tears stung her eyes. Clipped images of finding him in the woods, followed by their few interactions taunted her heart. She couldn't allow herself to dwell on the emotions they triggered. She knew her calling, and it wasn't Dillon's. His job was here with the family business.

The adjacent blank page challenged her. Emily moved her wrist to the top of the paper. Yet, she still couldn't bring herself to acknowledge her feelings out loud—or on paper. Instead of Dillon, the names of his niece and nephew appeared. Better to jot down their prayers and that of their family. But even as she wrote, flashes of Dillon's broad chest and shoulders teased her concentration.

Had he not recognized her? Enough time had passed since accepting the nanny position. Had he avoided her because he did remember? No. That didn't make sense. When she'd found Dillon, he'd only opened his eyes to look at her once. And then, he'd been in such pain she doubted he saw anything.

Nothing made sense, but things often didn't. The giddy feelings from finding him were enough, God would see to the details. She closed the journal and returned it to a shelf above the desk.

***

By morning, the rest of the house was awake and active by the time Emily descended the stairs for breakfast. Maurita smiled from beside the island counter and motioned to the plate of food at the table.

"Ah, *gracias*. You're so thoughtful."

The cook's smile widened as Spanish sentences rolled off her tongue.

Emily caught enough to understand she had been concerned. Maybe Dillon could explain to Maurita about last night. Or maybe the subject would be better left alone. As far as she knew, the children had been fast asleep and knew nothing of their mother's midnight visit.

Just as Emily finished the last of her orange juice, Maurita patted her arm and pointed toward Dillon's shop. "Eh, Dillon, you visit."

Emily absorbed the broken English. "Dillon wants me to stop by?"

"*Si! Si!*" Maurita's eyes brightened with joy.

Emily understood. Not able to express yourself to those you live around made a confining arrangement. She had often experienced the same. She understood isolation, and owed it to Maurita to brush up on her Spanish, and at the same time, help teach the cook more English.

Rhysa's and Jabali's English also needed work. She could teach them together. They'd start in the kitchen, naming items they came across. If made into a game, the children might join more readily, especially if she added a little competition to the mix.

Emily left the kitchen with renewed purpose. The comforting smell of fresh muffins faded into the building heat mixed with yesterday's mown grass. She inhaled deeply and followed the meandering path to Dillon.

A blast of hot air assaulted her as she stepped into the shop. Not even noon, and the temperature was already stifling. How could he stand working in here? She searched the building. Maybe he couldn't. Dillon wasn't anywhere she could see. The sound of a hammer against metal drew her eyes to the corner.

Emily weaved to the open door. Clad in a tight green t-shirt, Dillon stood poised to swing. She started to say something as the hammer made contact. She yelped and jumped back at the same time.

Dillon jerked his head up. His shirt highlighted the green in his hazel eyes. The heightened color did something funny to her stomach. His lips pulled in a handsome smile. "Good. Maurita must be doing better."

He swiped his face against his sleeve and together they walked toward the shade of a red bud. Dillon hooked his hand on the base of a limb above him. "Today's gonna be a scorcher."

"For you. The kids and I can stay in the house." Her smile came to a quick frown. Dillon's expression told her he had other plans. "What? No air conditioner?"

"We're going to the game. Be sure to pack plenty of water. We'll have to hit the road by ten."

"Don't we even get to vote? I'm really not much of a fan outside of the pajama department."

"We're meeting Robert." Dillon whispered this new bit of information then motioned her toward the shop.

Why were they meeting him? Wasn't he coming home? Once inside the over-sized furnace, Dillon expounded on the reason for the day's outing. "I thought it best if Robert didn't come home. We need to throw whoever it is off his trail and give us time to get a bearing on why all this is happening."

"You mean about Lainy—is she on his trail?"

Dillon frowned before his eyes widened with realization. "Oh, I talked to him after I'd said good-night to you. Someone tried to bump him into the opposite lane last night."

Emily's hand flew to her cheek. "Is he all right?"

"His car's got a battle scar, but he's fine. The police are trying to match the paint with the description

Robert gave. But since it was dark, I imagine it's another dead-end."

He rubbed a dirty finger against his temple, leaving a dark smudge. "He canceled his meeting and is on the way back."

"Why do we have to go to the game? Couldn't he come home for a while?" She raised her brows in a hopeful look. "It's cool in the house."

"No. I don't want anyone getting a lead on him. We won't even tell the kids we're meeting him there until we're well on the way."

***

Dillon scanned the crowd as he led the way to their seats. He didn't expect to recognize anyone, but watched for any unnatural interest toward the family. If Lainy sourced the attacks against Robert, she would've hired someone. Which meant the assassin wouldn't be easily recognized.

What was the reason behind this? He and Robert needed to have a long private talk.

Dillon stood to the side as Emily shuffled through the aisle to her seat, followed by Rhysa. Robert sat between his kids and Dillon took the end of the row. Both children beamed. While Jabali had yet to stop talking, Rhysa hadn't let go of Robert's hand. Emily mentioned Robert's continued absence would increase their insecurities. Judging by their clingy attachment to their dad, she was right.

Dillon preferred the role of uncle. Not overly demanding, he was often left alone to concentrate on work. But if Robert agreed to go into hiding until they determined who wanted him out of the picture, Dillon's position in the family would become a whole new ball game. He propped his elbow on the armrest with his chin resting in the crook of his thumb and forefinger. "I'm way out of my league."

Robert leaned over. "Did you say something?"

"No." He glanced down the row at Emily, and then muttered to himself, "Nothing I didn't already know."

The game picked up momentum and drew the avid attention of the crowd. The end of the first inning neared with the score tied at one. The pitcher threw for another strike but came in too close.

"Ball!" cried the ump.

Jabali stood and yelled with a crowd a few rows down. "Let him hit it!"

Dillon chuckled along with his brother. The little guy understood the game to perfection. The pitcher needed to trust his outfielders to handle the play. The pitcher spit on the mound then glanced at the seats. With a slight, almost unperceivable sign to the catcher, he threw a curve ball enticing the Red's batter to swing. The ball went high and to the left infielder. The Card's player jogged backward with his open glove held high above his head. Like a homing pigeon, the rawhide clapped into the mitt for a clean catch.

Jabali jumped up and down. "He heard me! The pitcher heard me!"

The horn sounded for the end of the first inning. Robert stood. "Time for snacks."

Dillon moved across the aisle to allow the family's exit.

Emily's amusement rang out above the rustle of the crowd. She trailed behind Rhysa but stayed engaged in conversation with her fans—three college-aged men.

Dillon took up the end of their small caboose. Emily paused to allow her new friends into their line, but Dillon ushered her forward. "Let's not get separated."

Although it was true, another reason fueled his action. A reason strangely resembling jealousy.

"Something wrong?" Robert leaned toward him as they waited in line for their food. His voice held a note of concern.

Dillon shook his head more from disengaging his thoughts from Emily than in answer to his brother. "Uh, no. Just thinking."

Robert wasn't slow. His eyes squinted from Dillon to Emily. Typical to his manner, a smirk pulled at the corner of his mouth, yet he withheld any comment. To Dillon, the common reaction irritated him more than if he'd said something.

Emily's strawberry blonde ponytail swung with a turn of her head. Their eyes locked. Dillon tried to frown and show disinterest. At the very least he should turn away. But instead, a smile tickled his lips. What happened to his self-control? Why couldn't he ignore her as he'd done when they first met? Right. He'd never been able to ignore her, only avoid her presence.

"Show Uncle Dillon. Do it. Make your face." Jabali whispered aloud to Emily.

She crossed her eyes and sucked in her cheeks. Dillon chuckled along with the children. Emily had a fun sense of humor. A man who'd been admiring her from the other line turned away. Good. There was a cure for her admirers. Maybe Dillon should try a childhood remedy and slap her on the back so her face would stay that way. Of course that would probably encourage her college-aged fans.

They made it back to their seats with hotdogs and sodas. Dillon viewed the overpriced snacks as enjoyable as the game itself. A quick look down the row revealed Emily's hotdog was nearly gone. She fit too perfectly with the family. Except with Lainy. But his brother's patience couldn't last forever. Eventually he'd see the real side of his wife and let her go.

Dillon gave one more glance toward Emily. He'd thought his heart had been broken a couple times in the past. But neither woman held the potential that Emily did. If he were smart, he'd keep his mind on his work.

Robert traded seats with Jabali. "I guess you got us here for a reason. You might want to discuss it before I get back into the game."

True. His brother was the largest Cardinals fan he knew. Well, next to Jabali.

"You need to take a vacation—a retreat." Dillon licked a blob of mustard off his finger then wadded the foil. "Maybe whoever's responsible for this will slip up quick and you won't have to be gone too long."

Dillon watched his brother's jaw set before he leaned forward. Robert rotated the wedding band on his finger. Something he always did while building a defense.

"Don't argue the logistics here. Someone cut your brake line, searched through your motel room, tried to run you into head-on traffic, and I think we can be certain my ordeal was intended for you." He tapped his recent scar.

Robert sighed and cast a glance toward Rhysa and Jabali—his main concern.

After the lives they'd both lived and then to be abandoned by their adoptive mom—Dillon knew leaving for a long period of time was the last thing his brother wanted to do.

"Even if I convinced myself they'd understand, I don't think their mental health is stable enough to really get it. If you thought my schedule was upsetting to them before, imagine how they'll respond to my complete absence." Robert, his big brother whose tireless energy always kept him upbeat, appeared almost beaten. He dropped his face in his hands.

Jabali started to speak when Emily's voice called his attention. Her attentiveness rivaled that of a saint.

Dillon picked at the curled lip of his cup. "I think they should've been told when I got hurt. Hiding it from them, not explaining the attempts against you now, only adds confusion."

"They'll be fine. We'll get to the bottom of this and they'll be fine. There's no other choice. Because like you said, if your injury was meant for me, it's only a matter of time before they're at risk, too." Robert straightened his back and reclaimed his usual got-it-all-together appearance. "But what about work? I can't just do nothing."

"Yes, you can. And it's important you do. Someone's been on to your every move. Take a retreat at the cabin. Who knows, it might do you some good."

***

Emily arranged the freshly peeled vegetables. She hoped the kids would be satisfied with the tray and yesterday's leftovers. After all she'd eaten while out, nothing sounded good for dinner.

A door slammed shut from upstairs. Footsteps thundered down the steps before Jabali wailed and ran down the hall. *What happened?*

Emily dropped the knife in the sink and located Jabali on his parent's bed. His knees were pulled to his chin, cheeks stained with tears. "My name is not Ubaya. I am Jabali!" He pumped his fist on his chest and cried harder.

Moving beside him, Emily wrapped her arms around the boy and hugged him close. He yelled out again, "I am Jabali." His voice lost its fervor and cracked under the pressure of emotion. He gave one last attempt, this time barely audible before crumbling in her lap. Heavy sobs racked his slight frame against her.

Emily eye's burned as she rocked back and forth. Rhysa's silence on the drive home had only been her temper building toward a storm. If there was a way to protect Robert at home, Dillon wouldn't have suggested he leave, but until they knew more, it seemed the logical explanation. Rhysa hadn't agreed. But she didn't have to take her frustrations out on her brother.

The boy's sobs turned to quiet weeping. Ubaya had been the name his birth mother had chosen. When translated, it meant bad feeling. She died shortly after his first birthday. Robert had explained that the father often reminded Jabali of his name's meaning, blaming him for his mother's death.

But Robert had it changed to Jabali—strong as a rock.

Emily softly hummed as she rubbed his back. Slowly, she added the words of the camp song she'd known since youth. *"You can talk about me just as you please. I'll talk about you down on my knees. All my sins been washed away I've been redeemed."*

Jabali stilled as she repeated the verse. Looking up, he asked, "What does that mean?"

Emily smoothed a hand over his cheeks, drying his tears. "It means when someone says something hurtful, give it straight to Jesus. Tell him about it and pray for the person."

He sniffed. "Why pray for them if they are mean?"

She swallowed. *Lord, please speak through me.* "Why do you think Rhysa lost her temper?"

Jabali's lip puckered as he looked away. Long slender fingers picked at the blanket. "Like me," his chest rose and fell with a shuddered sigh, "she is sad."

"Then don't you think she needs prayer?"

His eyes blinked rapidly before he gave a slow nod.

"You see, when someone says something hurtful, it's often because of one of two reasons. Either, they have hurt in their own hearts. Or, they don't have the peace that Jesus offers. Either way, they need our prayers."

He moved to his knees beside the bed. "Can we pray now?"

***

Emily doubled over as another pain sliced through her stomach. Had she gotten that stressed over the kids' upset or caught a bug? She swiped at the sweat on her forehead and grabbed the filled glass of water. She'd managed to get through most of the day feeling well. Why did the body always cave on a weekend, the evening at that? Another cramp set her off balance. She choked on the sip she'd taken and reached for the counter. The glass slipped from her hand and shattered on the floor.

Footsteps sounded on the stairs before Rhysa appeared in the doorway. "Are you okay?"

Emily moaned with pain and waved her back. "F-f-ine." She stumbled to the bathroom and closed the door. Another abdominal pain sent her to the floor.

Chapter Six

Dillon didn't usually take Saturdays off, and the ball game, though necessary, had cost him a day's work. He reached over the worktable and chose another piece of amber cut glass. The craftsman lampshade would fit perfectly into an arts and crafts home. The latest creation birthed from a combination of Japanese style lanterns and lighting from Frank Lloyd Wright. The cherry wood trim he'd stained would complete the piece.

The back door of the main house opened and slammed. Emily's pop-in visits weren't helping him get any work done. Since the day she was hired, Emily found excuses to seek him out. Whether it was a question about the children or merely coaxing him to the dinner table, her presence posed a constant distraction. A distraction he would welcome if it weren't for deadlines and her upcoming departure. He peeled off his louvers and swiped a hand over his face.

The children's smiling faces invaded his mind. Seated in the kitchen, they responded to Emily's jokes and found ways to mimic Dillon's mannerisms. The nanny's interruptions hadn't been for her own needs.

She was seeing to the needs of his niece and nephew. His selfish attitude had to change.

Footsteps neared along the rock path. Rhysa had been quiet since saying goodbye to Robert. Her silence had probably erupted by now, and Emily needed to vent.

Rhysa burst through the open doorway. "Uncle Dillon, Emily's sick." Worry lines creased her brow.

Dillon blinked in surprise. He hadn't expected his niece. "What do you mean she's sick?"

Moments after locking the shop, he stood outside the closed bathroom door and knocked for the third time. "Emily. I'm coming in." An unsettled feeling rose in his chest.

From inside came an unintelligible mumble. He turned to Rhysa. "When I open the door, you peek in and make sure she's decent."

Rhysa nodded, her eyes wide with concern. Regardless of the trial she'd been, Rhysa carried a large amount of compassion.

"She's on the floor!"

He pushed past his niece and dropped to his knees beside Emily. He smoothed away long hair that hid her face. She was so pale.

Dillon's heart hammered against his ribs. "Did you faint? Have you hit your head?"

A slight moan escaped her lips as her hand moved to her stomach. "Dunno. Cold tile feels good."

"I'm going to move you to your room."

"No. I'm too big."

Dillon slid his arms between Emily and the floor and drew her to his chest. "You're just right."

With Rhysa leading the way, he carried Emily up the stairs and to her bedroom. After his niece pulled down the bedding he turned to her, "Bring the trash can from the bathroom."

Jabali stood in the doorway. "I'll get it!"

Dillon felt reluctant to release Emily. At least in his arms he knew she was safe. Her pale coloring revealed a dusting of freckles over her nose. Pink lips flushed bright. Could she be feverish? Her eyes fluttered open followed by a painful moan. Dillon laid her gently on the bed and reached for the phone.

"Who are you calling?" Rhysa questioned him with fearful eyes. Her attachment to the nanny was evident.

"The nurse hotline." Dillon punched in the correct memory key his brother had programmed after receiving custody of Jabali. Between speaking with the nurse he asked Emily the routine questions.

"Sounds like you might have food poisoning." He stepped out long enough to bring back a wet washcloth for her forehead. "Let's go over what you ate today."

Emily moaned into the pillow. "I'd rather you not know."

Dillon smiled and touched her arm. True, she had a hearty appetite, but it was nothing to be embarrassed over. "You had a hot dog at the game and a bottle of water. Was that the last thing you ate?"

Jabali tapped him on the arm. "We had ice cream too, 'member?"

"Oh yeah, that was after the game." Had she eaten something intended for Robert?

"She had Dad's nachos, because he wanted something else."

That was right. They arrived early for batting practice. Robert's order had been messed up. Could someone have—nah. That was too much to assume. Yet, the far-fetched coincidence still goaded him.

"Stop talking about food. You're making me sick." Emily rolled toward the side of the bed and stood on shaky legs.

Dillon put an arm around her and helped guide her to the restroom. Once she was comfortably resettled, he sent the kids to bed and retrieved a glass of water for her nightstand.

"I'll stay in the house, just in case you need me."

Already, Emily's eyes were closed and her breathing relaxed with sleep. Their talk of food had been good medicine. Since returning from the bathroom, her skin had regained some of its color.

Dillon quietly closed the door. Rhysa slipped from her room. Had she been waiting this whole time?

"Will you stay in Dad's room?"

His heart softened. She and Jabali were so easy to love. "I'll do you one better. I'll sleep on the couch so I can hear if anything's needed."

"Thank you." Rhysa pulled back from the door before it closed with a soft click.

Maybe tonight's experience would have a positive effect on Rhysa and help her let go of the constant anger she carried. Dillon hoped.

At the bottom of the stairs, he stopped and stared at the office door. Fumbling through his keychain he found the latest addition.

Although Robert wanted to fix his marriage, he was aware of Lainy's certain weaknesses. Once she moved out, he'd changed the lock to his office.

Dillon entered the immaculate room so unlike his shop. In the bottom locked drawer were the files Robert had described. Finding the correct one, Dillon opened it on the desk and located the passwords he'd need to pay the company bills online.

He rubbed his temples with both hands. He'd never wanted to carry the burden of the business. Which is why he'd refused part ownership when their father had made the offer to both sons. Dillon was strictly the designer. The job paid well and left his mind free from the stress Robert's temporary absence now foisted on him.

He opened the Brewington's Lighting and Displays account. The balance sent him leaning back in the chair. Dillon swiped a hand over his face. He'd had no idea the business had done so well. Anytime his brother tried to discuss finances with him, Dillon changed the subject. To keep his mind open to design, he wanted his thoughts as free from distractions as possible. Evidently it had paid off.

The screen blinked back at him as if to stir his thoughts. Dillon rested his chin in his hand. Today's spotty conversations with Robert rolled through his mind. Between interruptions from the family, Robert had told him quite a bit.

Robert paid for Lainy's rent to keep her from making a hasty decision toward divorce. He wanted to give his wife room to breathe. Although she was the one who wanted Rhysa, none of them could have predicted the trial it would become. The stress had amplified smaller matters until time apart seemed a logical solution. Or at least one Robert was willing to accept.

But Dillon had to give his brother credit. He'd agreed to her time apart, but also stipulated if she wanted a separation then they would have separate accounts.

Dillon opened his brother's private account and typed in the amount to move into Lainy's. His heart grew heavy. The whole situation was a mess. One that happened every day all around the world.

After paying the few bills that were due, he closed the computer, locked the file drawer and the office door. The dollar amount from the business flashed in his mind like a neon sign. Who else knew the worth of Brewington's Lighting and Displays?

**

Emily awoke to the sun shimmering through her curtains. She smacked her dry lips relieved to see a glass of water sitting on her nightstand. A trashcan sat on the floor. Thankfully after her trip to the bathroom, she'd had no need of it.

She emptied the glass and sank back against the pillows. What could possibly have made her that sick? Nothing she'd eaten for breakfast had caused discomfort. She recounted her other meals. The realization tightened her stomach muscles.

She sat up, remembering the glass she'd dropped in the kitchen. Had someone swept the floor? Maurita may not see it—Jabali might cut his feet. She stared at the door then vaguely remembered Dillon carrying her upstairs. Warmth spread across her cheeks.

Emily pushed back the covers and stared at her rumpled appearance. At least she'd been fully clothed. But she wasn't a lightweight, and couldn't imagine what Dillon must think after the workout she'd caused him. Not that it mattered. She was here to serve the Lord, not the whims of her heart.

Acknowledging the tiny flame of attraction depressed her. Had the biblical Paul ever felt this way? Did the thorn in his side that he'd asked repeatedly be removed, originate from his heart?

The phone sat by her empty glass. Calling to cry on someone's shoulder in a moment of self-pity wasn't an option. Serving overseas most of her adult life didn't provide her with steady friends. And those she had, as missionaries themselves, were most often unreachable.

She could easily bare her disappointments to Mom, but as a mother, Ann would hang on to them too long, wishing she could somehow fix them. Emily's eyes moved to the small, framed photo of her and her siblings. Lined up on a log, their soaked clothing plastered their skinny bodies with smiles as wide as the creek. She couldn't bring herself to call her sister Lucy. She had enough on her plate with her sponsor child and father living on the farm.

Lucy and Dorin made a perfect couple and they weren't even aware of it yet. Emily bit her lip. *Help me not to envy them, Jesus.*

The sunrise transformed the white lace curtain over Emily's window into a brilliant orange. Shafts of light reached toward her bed like the hand of God. *Follow me*, He seemed to beckon. *I know what's best for you. Trust me always.*

The end of Emily's nose tickled as she fought the urge to cry. She always battled an emotional upsurge after being sick. She swiped a wayward tear. "I do trust you, God. That's why I keep going to the ends of the earth."

Her chest heaved with a huge sigh. "But I wish I didn't have to go alone."

***

Though it was Sunday, Emily didn't have need for a dress. The clock announced she missed her chance to drive home to share services with her family. She'd fallen back asleep during prayers which meant the

Brewington's had probably already left as well. She stood in front of the sparse closet and chose a pair of jeans and a faded, floral top.

Holding onto the railing for support, Emily descended the stairs. Her stomach was still sore and her body weak. If she could handle the smell of cooking, she'd probably benefit from a good breakfast.

Dillon stood from the table as she entered the kitchen. Surprised to see him home, Emily looked from him to the plates of eggs and bacon.

"Thought you might need some nourishment after last night."

Emily's stomach rumbled in response. "Thank you." She pulled out a chair and looked around the empty kitchen. "Where are the kids?"

"In their rooms studying. Since we missed church, I figured that was no excuse to miss a Sunday school lesson."

Emily admired the man seated across from her. He made a great uncle and would make a great father someday. Her heart did a pathetic patter.

She forced her attention back to the plate of food. Enthusiasm over the meal had died. The bland yellow of store-bought eggs lacked the flavor of free-range. But she'd never tell Dillon. His thoughtfulness meant a lot. Too much.

Dillon cleared his throat. Had he picked up on her mood? *Lord, forgive me for my selfishness. Help me to be grateful for all good things.*

"I know it's your day off, but if you don't have other plans, you could go with us to visit my dad."

"Your dad?" She hadn't considered the Brewington parents before now. "Where does he live?"

"Not far from here."

***

Soon after breakfast, Emily noted the sign at the entry where Dillon directed the car. Assisted living? Dillon's expression gave nothing away. Did he think Robert had already filled her in?

The front door opened into a homey sitting room. Residents seated in comfortable chairs greeted them with broad smiles. Emily had always held a fondness toward the elderly. Perhaps time would allow her to visit with some of the people before she left. More often than not, once family members entered facilities like this, their visitors greatly declined.

They stopped a few doors down the hall. A faint smell of bleach hung in the air. Two beds were in the spacious room. One rumpled, although currently vacant, the other bed was occupied.

"Hi Dad." Dillon moved to the man's side and pressed a kiss to his forehead before settling beside him in a chair. He nodded his head toward Emily and the children hovering by the door. "I brought you some company."

Confusion furrowed the man's brows as round eyes looked from Dillon to the doorway. Emily pressed a hand on Rhysa's and Jabali's backs to move them forward. When they refused, she stepped around them. "Hi Mr. Brewington, I'm Emily."

His face puckered to form a question before relaxing into a smile. He nodded and reached for her hand. Squeezing it gently, he then reached for Dillon's. With a clap, he joined their hands, one on top of the other. "Perfect fit. Like me and my Rose."

Emily blinked several times and tried to utter an explanation. The man's face lit with a sparkle making the truth harder to explain.

Dillon brought her hand closer to his side for a more relaxed hold. Emily fought to maintain a normal pattern of breathing. Did Dillon's palm not spark with a thousand tiny jolts of electricity?

"Thanks Dad." He cleared his throat. "Have you had a good day?"

The light slowly faded from his eyes. Mr. Brewington turned to the window. "Why do you call me Dad?"

The blood in Emily's veins went cold. Her heart ached for Dillon. Now she understood. His father suffered from memory loss. No wonder the children were uncomfortable. They didn't know how to deal with someone who couldn't remember them.

Dillon released her hand and reached for his father's. "I'm your son Dillon. It's okay if you don't remember. Are you getting enough to eat?"

Thank you, God, for Dillon's gentleness. Please give him strength as he deals with his dad's illness.

"Yes, I think so." His father peered at the door. "Who are they? Why are they staring at me?"

Rhysa immediately disappeared down the hall. Jabali looked back as though he wanted to follow. Emily touched Dillon's back. "Take your time. I'll take care of them."

***

Dillon rubbed his temple as Emily's footsteps faded from the room. His dad waved a finger in her direction. "That's the one for you, son. Don't let her slip away."

The light returned to his eyes as a smile stretched his dry lips. Whether he referenced Dillon as his son, or a figure of speech, didn't matter. To hear the term was enough.

Dillon opened his dad's closet. "Let's get you cleaned up for the day."

The nurses knew Dillon's routine. Each Sunday Mac's son would pick out his Sunday best and together they'd go to the cafeteria for lunch then take a stroll on the grounds.

"I heard your favorite is being served."

"Oh good. Possum stew!" His dad gave a mischievous snicker. The joke was something he rarely forgot, even if he couldn't connect it with his sons.

After his dress shirt was properly tucked, Dillon combed his dad's tousled gray hair. "Handsome as ever."

"Will my Rose be there?"

The often-asked question never failed to form a lump in Dillon's throat. He'd had yet to witness such love and devotion between two people as that of his parents. And it was the heartache of losing Mom that led to his father's stroke. "We're not meeting in the same place. But someday soon, Dad. Someday soon."

Dillon scanned the cafeteria for Emily and the kids. Although he didn't see them, he needn't worry. Emily was a complete professional.

He and Dad ate in comfortable silence and watched the other patrons at their tables, sometimes making small talk with those who passed. After their meal, Dillon cleared their dishes before following him outside.

Dad tapped Dillon's leg with his cane. "Do you still need to know where Robert is?"

As suddenly as if a coffin had slammed shut, Dillon's breath stalled and a chill settled over his chest. Who had asked his father the question? He had to think fast to stay ahead. "Sure. Where would he be?"

"He always enjoyed our cabin in the mountains. Why I remember Rose and I spending every Christmas there before the boys came along."

Every fiber of Dillon's body wanted to run. He had to contact Robert. But his brother left his smartphone with Dillon. And Dillon couldn't risk the children's safety by driving to the cabin to warn him, nor would Robert want him to.

His mind raced for a probable solution. He reached for his phone and looked up the number for the county sheriff nearest Robert.

Dillon guided his Dad to a bench. "Excuse me for a moment, Dad." He put enough space between them he wouldn't be overhead and explained the situation to the police station. He had to trust they'd get a warning to Robert. For now, it was all he could do.

Dillon returned to the bench. "Do you remember what I was wearing when I was here last?"

A half laugh tumbled from the aged man as he shook his head. "Now am I the one with a memory problem or are you?"

Residents scattered around the grounds. Some in wheel chairs, others walking or sitting. No one seemed out of place or sinister. Who could it have been? Dillon glanced at his watch. Time to find Emily. If someone could stop in and visit his dad, were any of them safe?

He saw his father back to his room. "Love you, Dad. I'll see you later."

"Take care of that sore throat, son."

Sore throat? Dillon didn't have a cold.

Chapter Seven

Emily gave in to the children's begging and donned her swimsuit. After yesterday's fiasco it would feel good to stretch her sore stomach muscles. Since visiting Mr. Brewington, the heat of the day steadily increased until it was too hot to do anything but swim.

Emily slipped into the cool water. She leaned back and let the water tickle her ears. She almost giggled as tingles raced to her hairline. Years had passed since she'd last lazed in a pool. A favorite summer past time, she'd forgotten how enjoyable the water could be.

Jabali poked her arm. "Do you know any games?"

Emily longed to swim laps, but water games could be equally as fun. "Let's play Marco Polo."

Jabali scrunched his brow. "Who's he?"

Emily smiled. "That's a history lesson for later. Right now it's just a game. I close my eyes and call *Marco*, while you two answer *Polo* and try not to get tagged."

The children caught on quickly and practiced throwing their voices to avoid being it. Emily yelled out, "Marco." Her call received giggles, minus the correct response of "Polo."

"Okay guys, this is my third time being it. By now you should know how to respond." Emily waded blindly in the water. "Marco."

She stretched her toes toward the bottom as her chin dipped under. Treading the deeper side of the pool, she called again. "Marco."

A strange sensation trickled along her skin. Not of panic, but trickery. She bumped into someone as giggles sounded from different sides of the pool. Emily opened her eyes.

Dillon!

She gasped and backstroked, receiving a mouthful of water. Emily sputtered and struggled her way to the side.

"We fooled you!" Jabali ran along the side of the pool, water streaming down his swim trunks and legs.

Dillon swam to her side. "Um ... Polo."

"Cute." She faced him and caught her breath in her throat. His eyes, like a forested hillside, ranged in different depths of dark and light green. She could get lost in them and never reach the other side.

She forced her eyes downward. But his thick chest and muscled arms provided more distraction. The hours Dillon spent swinging a hammer had definitely benefited his physique. His smile penetrated through the fog of her senses. She forced her attention back toward his face, though off centering it enough to include Jabali.

"Come on, Jabali." Dillon held out his arms. "Jump and I'll throw you in."

The boy jumped without hesitation into his uncle's arms. Dillon tossed him toward the deep side of the pool ending in a big splash.

He soon broke the surface and yelled, "Again! Again!"

Dillon replayed the game several more times before Rhysa's prolonged silence signaled Emily's natural alarm. She searched the perimeter.

Seated behind them, the girl's concentration centered on Dillon's shoulder. A look of horror shadowed her gaze. Yet beneath the fear, stirred something else. The furrow in her brow deepened.

"Uncle Dillon." Rhysa hugged her arms around her waist. "What happened?"

Water splashed in Emily's face as Jabali returned to the side. Enjoyment faded from the boy's eyes as he examined Rhysa then his uncle. The air tensed with the children's uncertainty.

Dillon swiped the water from his face before flattening his palms on the concrete deck. His muscles corded along his arms as he hoisted himself from the pool. Rivulets of water raced down his length. He grabbed a towel and proceeded to dry off, obviously giving thought to how he should answer.

Emily stayed by the side of the pool. The children didn't already know? She held her breath, waiting to hear how he would explain the truth without scaring them.

Dillon's chest expanded with air. "I was hurt a few months ago. But you know that."

Emily climbed from the pool then helped Jabali out.

Rhysa didn't move. "I've not always lived here. I know what a scar from a bullet looks like." She ran a tongue over her lips. Her eyes darted around the pool.

Jabali touched Dillon's arm. "You hurt yourself in the shop. Right?"

Emily wanted to escape. The brothers' secrecy hadn't included her, but would the children understand? She sought an excuse, but nothing came to mind. *If this is where I'm supposed to be, Lord, then show me how to help.*

"I didn't hurt myself in the shop." Dillon looked from each child. "I was shot."

Jabali's hand slid from Dillon's arm. He stepped backward into Emily. A slight tremor vibrated through his slim form.

Dillon pulled out a chair from the outdoor table and sat down. His gesture was important as it showed the children he was willing to talk and answer their questions.

Emily took Jabali's hand. "Let's take a seat, too."

Rhysa didn't move. As if there wasn't a soul in the world she could trust, she didn't budge. Her eyes clouded with doubt.

Dillon rubbed his temple. He connected with Emily's gaze then released a sigh. "I was shot while hunting. Maybe it was a stray bullet, maybe not."

Emily understood his difficult situation. He didn't want to fill the children with fear, yet at the same time Rhysa's doubts made it clear she and Jabali needed to understand the situation.

Dillon dragged a finger back and forth on top of the table. The action created a fast thumping sound over the woven metal. "Someone wants to harm our family. There've been … certain incidents … that have made it important your dad stays away for a while. We don't want what happened to me in the woods, happening to him."

Rhysa looked away. A few moments passed before she spoke. "Is it Mom?"

"Is what your mom?"

"I know about Dad's car. I heard you talking with him when it happened." She pinned her uncle with a steady stare. "Is Lainy trying to kill Dad?"

Emily swallowed and looked back at Dillon. The girl's worries mirrored her own.

"No—I … I don't know who is." Dillon rose from the table. "But don't worry. I won't let anything happen to you. Any of you—including your dad." Without another word, he set off toward the cottage.

The poor man. He'd been thrust into more responsibility than he knew how to handle. Emily ushered the kids inside. "Let's get dressed."

She should offer an outing, something. But the mood of the household had taken a turn. The best thing she could do was spend time with God. Different passages of scripture floated to the surface, *"thine alms are had in remembrance … thy words were heard …"* God always heard the prayers of His children. They would all benefit from time alone with Him.

Alone in her room, Emily bowed her head. *Guard Rhysa's heart and the power of her emotions with the breastplate of Your righteousness, God. Let it filter out the things that would draw her attention further from You by making her angry or sad. Strengthen her by impressing the workings of Your Spirit into her heart. And last of all help her feel secure.*

An hour later Emily opened the refrigerator to consider what to make for dinner. She pulled out the vegetable drawer to rummage through. *A salad might be—*

"Emily!" Jabali rushed into the room.

Emily raised her head too quickly and hit the bottom of the freezer door. "Ow. What is it Jabali?" She grimaced and rubbed the sore area.

"Rhysa's gone."

What did he mean gone? Emily's stomach turned to stone. Gone as in took a walk or gone as in ran away? "Have you searched the house?"

He nodded rapidly.

"I'll take a look, too. If I can't find her, we'll have to tell your uncle."

Emily didn't wait for Jabali's response but rushed through the downstairs, looking behind furniture as she went.

Constant turmoil kept Rhysa coiled like a snake. And why not? As a Ukrainian orphan, she'd taken four different trips to the U.S. under a sponsorship designed to match orphaned children with families wanting to adopt. After the five or six week stay, Rhysa would return to the Ukraine with hopes of adoption. Each family rejected her. Until Robert and Lainy. And now she chanced losing them.

Emily wished she could fix it all. Take away the girl's hurts, her unworthy feelings, her rejection.

The second story proved as empty as the main floor. Anxiety tensed the muscles along Emily's back as she returned to Jabali. "Go tell Uncle Dillon. I'll search the field."

If Rhysa visited the shop, Emily would hear before going too far. But something told her this game of hide and seek wouldn't be that easy.

She heard Dillon's voice behind her.

"We'll check the bus stops." He caught up and handed her a phone. "This is Robert's. I'll call if we find her. You do the same. My number's in there."

Emily tucked the phone in her pocket as they went their separate ways. Had Dillon expected his niece's disappearance? His lack of hesitation suggested as much. If only things were different with Lainy. Couldn't the woman see how much hurt she'd caused? A small voice whispered in the back of Emily's mind, *"Not if her thoughts were only on the money."*

It couldn't be true. Although they'd only met once, Lainy hadn't seemed like the type of person capable of murder. Nor did she look like the type that could handle a long-range rifle, like the one that shot Dillon.

A chill sent goose bumps along her arms. She had to find Rhysa.

The field proved as empty as it was hot. Emily swiped her brow and pulled her hair away from her neck. Fanning a breeze to cool her skin, she ventured into the woods. The shade offered a reprieve from the intense heat, but little else. Emily's clothes clung from the humidity and the underbrush scratched against her bare legs making them itch. "Rhysa, where are you?"

Every tree, every blade of grass, took on the same appearance. Her body temperature rose with anxiety, but she couldn't allow worry to blind her from the obvious. *Show me a path, God. There has to be a place she goes, some place familiar.*

Feeling a pull to change her course, Emily turned. Within a few yards she located a foot trail. "Thank you, Jesus." Although it was still early in the evening, she continued to hurry.

The further she walked, the larger the trees became. Emily soon came to a creek. Following the trickle of water, she spotted a red shirt in a large hickory.

"Go away." The flat response sounded from above.

Emily sighed and leaned against the tree's trunk. *Finally, she'd been found. Thank you, God.* "We're going to talk, but first I have to tell your uncle he can stop searching." She withdrew the phone from her pocket.

"He—he's looking for me, *too*?"

Tears formed in Emily's eyes. Rhysa's small-voiced question revealed how worthless she saw herself.

Emily scrolled to the D's.

A man answered abruptly. "Robert! Where are you? I've been trying to reach you."

"Oh, I'm sorry." The exertion and heat tired Emily. She didn't sound like herself. "I dialed the wrong number."

"Lainy—this isn't you."

Emily's heart stilled. Her skin prickled with alarm.

As quickly as the red flag appeared, the warning left. "No, I'm Emily, the Brewington's nanny. I really have to go. Sorry for the mistake." She hung up and found Dillon's name.

After the call to Dillon, she slipped the phone back inside her pocket and reached for the lowest branch.

Rhysa snorted. "You'll only hurt yourself."

Emily threw a leg over another branch and pulled herself up beside Rhysa with the skill of a youth. "Or maybe not. I grew up climbing trees."

Rhysa rolled her eyes and turned away.

"I had a special place like this, too, on my parent's farm."

Rhysa picked a loose piece of bark. "You grew up on a farm?"

Emily's heart gave a hopeful leap. *God, help me break through to her.* "Yes. They still live there and raise cattle. But they also have some pigs and chickens."

A hinted smile brightened the girl's features.

Emily pulled a leaf off a branch and used it as a map. "Here was our cabin—"

"You lived in a cabin—like a log cabin?"

Emily nodded, a bit surprised by the sudden interest.

Rhysa broke the bark in her hands into pieces. "I read a book once about a boy who lost a mitten. All kinds of animals snuggled in the mitten together until it was stretched out."

"I think I've read that book." But what did that story have to do the Durham home?

"The boy and his baba lived in a cabin." Rhysa watched the crumbs of bark fall to the ground below. "I used to wish I was him. To have a cozy, warm home. A grandma that would make me mittens. And many animals around our home."

"That sounds nice." Emily yearned to understand Rhysa. "Did you ever wish for a mother, too?"

"No." The response fell from her lips with too much ease. "Moms always leave."

Emily traced the leaf with her finger. "My mom did, too."

Rhysa spun to look at Emily, but the quick motion unbalanced the preteen. She sucked in air and grabbed at an upper limb—and missed. Rhysa's wide eyes enlarged in panic and she warbled a strangled cry.

Emily lunged sideways and locked her hands around the girl's wrists.

Rhysa scraped at the tree with her feet until a foot hooked a branch. With a surge of energy, she heaved herself back on top of the limb.

They both took a deep breath of relief then Rhysa released a nervous chuckle. "That hasn't happened before."

"Good." Emily stroked her fingers down the side of Rhysa's face. "I hope it never does again."

Like an inner-city subway drummer, Emily's heart kept a hard, fast beat. She leaned against the trunk until it slowed. "Let's get down and start walking back before your uncle comes looking for us both." Arm over arm, Emily swung to the ground then Rhysa followed.

As the woods merged into field, Rhysa picked up where they left off. "Why did your mom leave?"

A strand of hair came to rest on Emily's lashes. She blew a puff of air toward it and wished for a ponytail. "Sometimes people have problems they keep hidden on the inside, where others can't see."

She stooped and pushed back the tall grass, revealing the ground below. "It's like this dirt. We assume from what's growing in the field that its good soil, but we never fully know until it's tested. Only then do we learn if it's depleted of important minerals.

"People are like that, too. Sometimes they lack the right balance of chemicals. But if they're willing and able, doctors can often help them."

Rhysa chewed on her bottom lip. "Did your mom not want help?"

Emily shrugged. "I was young when she left, so I don't know. But God knew I still needed a mother, because He sent us a wonderful woman named Ann."

"God doesn't care about me." Rhysa plucked a blade of grass and tore it down the vein. "He never has."

A lump lodged in Emily's throat. She couldn't imagine not feeling God's love. "Have you tried talking to Him?"

"Yes. And I know people say He answers every prayer. But I think He forgets mine."

Emily shook her head. "He doesn't forget, but sometimes He has us wait." She knew any explanation she gave wouldn't be enough to counter Rhysa's years of neglect.

A rabbit bounded into the field unaware of their presence. Rhysa's attention fixed on the rodent as it bent its head to graze. The only visible part left was its long ears.

They continued toward the house. Alerted to their presence, the rabbit's head rose above the grass. His little nose twitched back and forth before bounding for safety.

Emily watched Rhysa's sad face. She wanted to assure her of God's love, but experience taught her that in matters of faith, people couldn't be rushed. Seeds were being planted. God would do the watering.

They were almost to the yard when a high-pitched shrill came from the woods. Rhysa squealed and grabbed Emily's hand. "What was that!"

Chapter Eight

Emily strained to see the source of the shriek. Something small darted through the grass in a zigzag pattern. But what didn't dart bothered her. Two furry dogs with black bands across their tails growled and snapped at one another before giving chase to the rabbit. Coyotes.

Rhysa gasped and took off in a run.

Emily caught up and pulled her to a stop. "Don't run. You'll only look like game. I'll keep an eye on them while we walk to the house." Although coyotes rarely attacked humans, they were capable of the crime and not to be trusted.

"Are they following us?" Rhysa fumbled for Emily's hand.

With another glance behind them, Emily answered, "No. They went the opposite direction."

Rhysa's hand tightened. "Thank you for coming for me." A tremor shook her voice.

Touched by her show of emotion, Emily pulled her into a side embrace. Rhysa released a sob and swiped her eyes. "What about the rabbit?"

"I'm sure the rabbit found safety." For Rhysa's sake, Emily hoped it hadn't sustained a serious injury. She rubbed the girl's back thankful they weren't harmed. "Still think God doesn't care for you?"

Rhysa shrugged. "Too many times He hasn't. What is it that they say? I'm a little fish in a big pond."

They reached the house as the door flew open. Dillon and Jabali rushed out. Dillon pulled Rhysa into his arms for a tight embrace then released her. "Don't do that again." His command was followed by a quick sigh and shake of his head. "We couldn't bear to lose you."

A sheen of moisture glimmered in Rhysa's eyes before Jabali's long, slender arms surrounded her waist. She returned his squeeze and whispered, "Sorry, brother. I'm sorry."

Dillon swiped a hand over his face. The hour of worry had momentarily aged him. Weary lines etched his eyes and mouth.

"Rhysa," Emily patted her back, "why don't you and Jabali call in a couple of pizzas. We'll make dinner easy."

She stopped at the door with her head turned but downcast and spoke barely above a whisper. "Sorry, Uncle Dillon."

"Me too." He patted his scar.

Emily was sure Rhysa understood that he, too, was sorry for keeping secrets.

The door closed and Emily directed Dillon's attention toward the field. "What draws the coyotes so close? Your cat doesn't stray far from the shop, does he?"

"No. And most of the time he talks me into letting him sleep in the carrier inside." He scratched his head. "Coyotes? Did you see any?"

"Yes and too close. They were after a rabbit."

Dillon turned down the path. "I'll be back for dinner."

Emily stayed by the door, unwilling to leave Dillon completely alone.

Coyotes had never been a problem on the farm. But the vast countryside offered more game than the confines of suburbia.

Dillon entered the field and faded behind the security fence. What was he looking for? Wild animals weren't that uncommon.

Happiness bubbled from inside the house. The children had settled down and were back to being kids. Good. Their life needed normalcy. Images of Lainy floated to the surface. Was she interested in fixing her marriage at all? If not, what goals kept her occupied?

Dillon returned to the yard. Emily met him halfway. "Did you find anything?" The scowl on his face said he had.

"Someone's been dumping garbage over the fence."

Garbage, pet food, water dishes, they were all sources of interest to coyotes. "One of your neighbors, maybe?"

Dillon shrugged. "Maybe. I'll talk with some of them."

Although the idea was possible, the act would take any neighbor out of their way. The fence didn't begin until the back yard, which meant whoever was doing the dumping had to trespass through the front.

Dillon touched Emily's arm and drew her to a stop. Warmth spread to her cheeks just as before when Mac Brewington had pressed their hands together. "Where did you find Rhysa?"

"Down by the creek, in a hickory tree."

He glanced in the direction of the creek. "We'd better make sure she sticks closer to home. Especially until we know Robert's safe."

"I agree. By the way, I've been meaning to ask," Emily lifted her hair off her neck and tossed it back, "does Lainy visit your dad?"

Dillon's eyes narrowed. "Not that I'm aware of."

Emily moved toward the house, enticing Dillon to follow. She didn't want to be away from the children for long. "A nurse mentioned how nice it was that he received such regular visitors like you and his daughter-in-law."

A fog of confusion wrapped around Dillon's features. Nothing made sense, and nothing would make sense until they talked to Lainy. "Talk to her, Dillon. Find out what's going on."

Dillon nodded as his phone rang in his shirt pocket. He glanced at the screen before pinning Emily with an incredulous stare. "Speak of the devil."

The phrase made Emily cringe. She moved to give Dillon privacy. His hand reached out and held her in place. He turned toward the shop then back to the house. Dillon's hand slid down Emily's arm with his movements, but he didn't let go. Whatever was happening, they were in this together.

"You want to what?" Disbelief furrowed Dillon's brow. "Why now? What—"

"I'll check with them and give you a call back." Another moment of silence followed as Dillon waited for Lainy to speak. "No, it's entirely fair. They have a right to choose."

Dillon snapped the phone shut. His hand moved from Emily's arm to her back as they advanced toward the door. Although she'd never wish for the upsets that spurred Dillon's need for contact, she cherished the results.

He paused before entering the house. "Lainy wants time with the kids. She'd like to have them tomorrow."

"What?" A surge of protection toward the children reared inside her. She'd prayed the woman would reclaim her interest in the children, but it was too unexpected. "What's her motive?"

"Exactly."

Inside, Dillon gathered the kids in the sitting room as they waited for the pizza delivery. He rubbed his temples with both hands. Emily had grown accustomed enough with his habits she knew he struggled with where to begin.

She sat forward, wanting to jump in and take over, yet hesitated. It wasn't her place. But if Dillon showed any doubts in their mother, or lack of respect, the children were likely to emulate his opinion. Emily caught his attention as he looked up. With a tip of his head, he gave her the okay.

She cleared her throat. "How would you two feel about spending time with your mom tomorrow?"

Silent, questioning faces looked at her in surprise. Rhysa was the first to respond. "Why?"

Emily put off answering until Jabali had expressed himself. "What do you think, Jabali? Do you miss your mom?"

He shrugged a thin shoulder. "She hasn't been here for so long, I don't know."

The doorbell rang stalling an answer and announcing dinnertime. Dillon reached for his wallet to pay the deliveryman. "Thanks."

Everyone followed him and the smell of melting cheese and Italian sauce into the kitchen. Despite the conversation, the children's moods didn't seem affected.

Working together they set the table with plates and napkins then waited while Dillon said grace.

"… and Father, we seek Your wisdom in the decisions that need to be made. Amen."

Jabali bit into his slice and spoke around the food. "I say we go. We can always say no the next time." His eyes darted toward his sister.

Rhysa rolled her eyes. "Okay. Maybe we'll find out some stuff."

"Stuff—like what?" Dillon's face stilled as he waited for her answer.

"Just things I've wondered about."

Emily traded glances with Dillon but remained silent. Rhysa would talk in her own time. Most likely after coming home from Lainy's.

The table conversation turned into the usual light-hearted mimicking of Dillon. Jabali was the first to start rubbing his temple. He then tried an impression of his uncle's voice, the best he could around his African accent. This sent Rhysa into a fit of giggles drawing Emily into the fun.

The happy atmosphere continued to grow as they finished eating and cleared the table. Perhaps it was the adrenaline rush of the day finally coming to an end.

Jabali rinsed his plate then turned the sprayer onto his uncle. A hoot sounded from Dillon before he blocked the stream with his plate. As he advanced toward the sink, Jabali worked the sprayer in too many directions for Dillon to deflect, soaking his jeans and shirt.

Jabali's white teeth showed brightly as his head bobbed with laughter. His eyes darted toward the sitting room before Dillon lunged toward him. He yelped and twisted to the side. Despite how hard he wriggled he couldn't escape. Dillon locked him in a hold with one arm while giving his ribs a good tickle.

Emily pictured herself in Dillon's arms the night she was sick. Had he treated her as he would've anyone, or had he relished the chance to hold her close? Too bad she couldn't remember what it had felt like. Warmth spread across her cheeks.

The tickle war came to a close as Dillon and Jabali caught their breath. Emily grabbed a towel to clean up the water mess while Rhysa helped with the dishes. But the distraction wasn't enough to free Emily's mind. Did Dillon ever revisit the memory? Probably not. Nor did she need to. Thinking of a type of romantic relationship was futile when she'd be far away in only a few short months.

God had made her calling clear. There were so many hurting, lost souls, and she'd been blessed with the position to help them.

Dillon's good-humored voice carried after Jabali's into the back yard. Why did a simple summer job have to include a man that confused her? Did God allow this to prove her devotion to her calling? She often saw the spiritual battle of situations around her, but this time proved challenging. Could Satan have orchestrated this distraction?

**

Emily said goodnight to each child and headed for her own room. Before she closed the door she heard her name called.

"Emily." Rhysa stood in the hallway, her eyes rimmed with red. Although it didn't look as though she'd been crying, emotions were near the surface. "Don't forget to pray for the rabbit."

Emily retraced her steps. "Do you have a pen?"

Rhysa nodded and reached toward her dresser.

"Hold out your hand." Emily wrote "bunny" in bold letters on Rhysa's palm and then on her own. "Now every time we see that word, we'll say a prayer. I think you'll be surprised how often you remember that furry fish in the big 'ole grassy pond."

***

Dillon parked in front of Lainy's apartment. He walked the kids to the front door and gave Rhysa a trac phone he'd picked up that morning. "I programmed this already. Call if you need me."

He glanced from each child's face. Eagerness sparked in Jabali's eyes. He hoped they weren't disappointed.

Lainy opened the door without any flair. Good sign. At least she wasn't putting on airs for the children. She smiled and hugged Jabali. "Good to see you." Then her attention centered on Rhysa. "I'm happy to see you, too."

Rhysa remained silent and turned back to Dillon. She sighed heavily. "I'll see you later."

Dillon hadn't expected how hard it would be to leave. He leveled a look toward Lainy. She lowered her head a fraction before easing the door closed. At least she understood he wasn't comfortable, perhaps that would make her more careful with the children's hearts.

So this is what it felt like to be a dad. Having lost hope in marriage, Dillon had also given up on the possibility of fatherhood. A part of him always struggled with the decision, but he didn't want to risk a broken home. And there were enough examples of broken marriages to outweigh any lasting ones he might encounter.

He drove through the business district, not ready to go home in case the phone rang and the children already wanted to come back. Swim tubes and water toys were displayed outside of several stores to draw in buyers. Dillon surprised himself by pulling into a parking lot. Since when had the children monopolized this much of his time ... or his heart?

He returned to the truck with his arms full of snorkeling gear and water games. Not that they needed either. Robert provided well for them and snorkeling in the pool couldn't be very entertaining. Still, Dillon's spirits lifted doing something for them.

What would Emily think of his spontaneous purchases? He could hear her hearty laugh explode. And he'd join in. Her buoyant personality had a way of drawing people to her.

Dillon pulled around to the back of the house. He'd given Emily the day off to visit her family since she missed Sunday and didn't expect her back until late. Should he wrap the gifts or set them out, ready to use?

"Wow, what'd you buy? Is that a blow-up seal?" Emily met him in the yard. "I could never stay on one of those things. But it never stopped me from trying."

A foreign sensation traveled through Dillon's body. Whatever it was, it felt satisfying. Emily's eyes sparkled like diamonds as she looked from him to the items he carried. Dillon swallowed hard. *Don't let me lose my heart here, God. She's leaving. You know that.*

"I thought I sent you home."

"You did. But I decided to stay. You know, just in case the kids ..."

"Yeah, I know."

The understanding was mutual. Neither of them was comfortable with the arrangement. Emily tugged on the seal package. "I'll blow this up."

The compressor in the shop would do a faster job, especially considering the seal wasn't the only thing needing air, but Dillon didn't object. It would be an excuse to stay in each other's company.

After resting their jaws from the inflatable toys, Emily returned to the shaded veranda with two glasses of cold lemonade.

Dillon turned the glass in his hand. "What's with all the fruit?" Frozen blueberries, strawberries and raspberries floated among the ice.

"It's something I picked up while traveling. Different fruit was used, but this is what we had on hand."

Traveling. Like he needed the reminder she wasn't for keeps. He took a long swig and allowed the sugar to mellow him before asking the dreaded question. "Where are you headed next?" *Please say somewhere close.*

"Kurdistan." A softness infused her voice.

Her answer fell like a weight to the bottom of his heart. Did her gentle tone mean she also dreaded her departure, or was the wistfulness from her passion for the people?

"What will you do there?"

"I'm still not sure. I mean, I know I'm supposed to work with the Kurds, but the details are fuzzy." Emily tossed her hair behind a shoulder and stared off into the field, seeming to stall for time.

"They're a despised people without any borders of their own. One of their proverbs says, "*The Kurds have no friends but the mountains.*" They feel the world has forgotten them. I want to help change that."

Dillon didn't understand. But he also didn't want to dwell on the subject. He clenched his teeth, resisting the urge to rub his temple. If the children knew to mimic his small habits, then Emily probably understood him more than he'd like.

Three hours had passed since dropping the kids off at their mom's. Dillon reached for his phone. It wouldn't hurt to check.

His pulse skipped a beat as he glanced at the screen. How did he miss Rhysa's call? His stomach clenched as he tapped her recorded number.

Rhysa picked up on the first ring. "Uncle Dillon, we're ready to come home. Now."

Chapter Nine

Dillon stood too fast and toppled his chair. His heart raced as long strides took him toward the truck. "Why—What's wrong, Rhysa?" Emily kept pace by his side.

"She's—" A phone rang from somewhere in Lainy's apartment. Rhysa's voice softened to a whisper. "Just a minute."

He started the truck as Emily fastened her seatbelt. He shouldn't have let them go. Lainy wasn't trustworthy. Had she only invited them over to try to pin Robert's location? The idea hadn't entered his mind until now. But she had to know the children couldn't keep up with their dad's schedule. Unfortunately, neither could Dillon. The conferences often connected his brother with company heads and their distributors. One meeting would turn into several, securing the company's growth and Robert's absence from home.

Robert often stayed at the family cabin rather than return home if there wasn't enough turn around between meetings. But if whoever had visited their dad knew where the cabin was ... Dillon couldn't dwell on that now. First he had to protect the kids. *God, Robert's in Your hands. Prepare him for what's ahead and defeat the enemy's plans against him.*

Although Rhysa wasn't speaking directly to Dillon, her voice came across the phone loud enough for Emily to hear.

Emily raised her brows. "What's she yelling about?"

He shook his head and handed Emily the phone. "Something to do with Lainy lying and using them. Let's just hope she doesn't throw the phone. I shouldn't have let them go."

"And how could you have stopped them? Lainy's their legal mother."

Dillon grimaced and kept his eyes on the road. Emily was right, which meant he couldn't risk losing his temper. Legally, she could run over his heart as easily as Robert's but by a different route—by use of the kids.

He sighed and flipped on his blinker. If Robert didn't call this evening, then Dillon would find a way to contact him, even if he had to go through the county sheriff. The door to the apartment flung open as Dillon pulled into the drive. Lainy rushed out after the children. Her explanation tumbled off her lips as he exited the cab. "Rhysa misunderstood a simple phone call."

The children passed Dillon and filed into the back seat as Emily held the door open. Anger clenched his jaw. He wasn't a violent man, but Lainy could tempt even the calmest of saints. "You only had them for three hours." The words ground out between his teeth.

"You know how Rhysa's temper gets out of control. I'm surprised she held it in check for as long as she did."

Dillon rubbed his brow trying to dissuade a building headache. "What I know is how the two of you work around each other so don't treat me as if I'm clueless. What triggered it?"

"Mind your own business." Her chin rose in defiance. "The little tiff was between mother and daughter. Leave it there."

"You know I won't." Disgusted, he made to leave and stopped. "Lainy, what happened to the woman my brother married?"

She blinked away an instant sheen in her eyes and cocked her head. Too soon, the thoughtful moment was replaced by her usual façade. "I changed."

He gave one last thoughtful stare. "Be careful you don't go so far, you can't come back."

Dillon pulled onto the road and glanced in the rearview mirror. Jabali sat slumped against the window with a broken heart while fire flickered in Rhysa's eyes and colored her cheeks. What could've taken place?

"Some guy wants Mom to move in with him." Rhysa met Dillon's eyes as he whipped his gaze toward her then back to the road.

"Who? How did you find out?"

"I heard her on the phone."

Thoughts collided in Dillon's mind like a five car pile-up. Could their suspect be working with Lainy? Was she capable of such evil? "How do you know it was a man? It could have been a woman friend."

Rhysa scoffed. "Body language says it all."

He glanced toward Emily. She lifted a palm up as though she didn't understand any more than him.

Dillon pulled up to the cottage and parked, uncertain what to do next. Should he suggest Jabali help him in the shop? The boy hadn't said a word since they picked him up. What thoughts were occupying his mind?

"What's in there?" Jabali pointed toward the veranda as he slipped from the truck and ran toward the inflated seal.

"Why don't you look and see." Dillon smiled, not only because of the boy's enthusiasm but also from relief. The gifts saved him from an awkward position. Although he still wanted to understand what happened, learning about it under the natural ease of goofing off in the pool was much more appealing than suddenly asking Jabali for help.

Had he ever asked either child to work with him? The truth disturbed him. Lost in his own selfish realm, he kept himself distant from the world and ultimately his family. How would he feel to be young and not have anyone to trust? Both children's lives had revolved around sorrow and rejection. And leaving the job in their adoptive parent's hands, Dillon had done nothing to help.

He swallowed against a sudden lump of regret. It was time to change.

Jabali squealed in excitement. "Water toys!" A glow of shiny white teeth helped prove his appreciation.

If the boy could move past hurt this easily, why should his uncle hold him back? Dillon ran after Jabali, passed him, and leapt into the pool, clothes and all.

***

Emily watched with fascination as Dillon changed from a tightly wound cord to a slippery fish. What had happened in the last few minutes?

She turned to Rhysa. Whatever it was, the impression hadn't been strong enough to persuade the troubled girl.

"Come on." Emily tugged on her hand. "I found some pictures while cleaning the basement. I think you might find a few you'll want in your room."

Rhysa stiffly trudged beside her. "Why would you clean the basement?"

"Because between Maurita and me, the rest of the house was spotless. But I was still restless."

Intelligence lit Rhysa's light blue gaze. "Are you still?"

Emily knew a part of Rhysa's security rested in her answer. "No. Not since you and your brother came home."

A glow softened Rhysa's features. But it wouldn't last. Emily was determined to learn what happened at Lainy's.

She didn't have to wait long. They passed Robert and Lainy's bedroom before reaching the door to the basement. Rhysa stopped and glared from one corner of the room to the other. "She reminds me of Ms. Boiko from the orphanage."

Emily assumed the "she" spoken of was meant for Lainy, but didn't want to interrupt and chance Rhysa withdrawing.

Rhysa's eyes took on a faraway look as she entered her past. "She would bring out special dresses and ribbons for Olga and Tamara. Never me." Her eyes dropped to her frame. "She only wanted pretty girls."

Wishing Rhysa could see her own beauty and worth wouldn't make it come true. From now on, Emily would make a point to build the girl's confidence.

Emily's eyes stung. She hugged her arms around her waist to keep from reaching out. There would be time for consoling later. Right now Rhysa needed to vent and trust Emily with the haunts of her past.

"Then she would tell them what to say when the *vazhlyvyy*—the um …" she stalled as if searching for the correct American word, "*important* people came.

"The girls even had to smile and hug her." Her eyes fell flat. "It was so fake."

"Where were you during this?"

"In the basement. But sometimes I would sneak up and watch."

"What do you mean the basement?" Emily had toured enough orphanages to know this couldn't mean a good place.

"There were too many of us. Ms. Boiko would get into trouble if they found out. So we extras had to hide and be real quiet until we were told the *vazh*—I mean, important men were gone."

Emily searched Rhysa's eyes. Although resentment hardened her voice, the fear she expected to see wasn't there. Instead, strength stared back.

Rhysa tossed her head. "Don't feel pity for me."

"Oh, hon'." Emily pulled her into a hug. "Never pity. Only admiration."

Rhysa returned a short squeeze before backing out of Emily's embrace. Of course, Rhysa wasn't comfortable with that much affection. She'd probably lived most of her life without hugs.

She tilted her head. "Why admiration?"

"Because of your strength."

"Oh." The response fell flat as Rhysa glanced at her arms.

Emily put a finger beneath her chin, bringing it up a notch. "I wasn't talking about physical strength. I meant the kind that comes from within. A strength that stays determined and fights for what's right."

A smile melted some of Rhysa's tension. Emily opened the basement door. "Let's take a look at those pictures."

Downstairs, Emily stopped near a stack of pictures leaning against the basement wall. She lifted the one in front. "Aren't these flowers pretty?" They would add color against her white walls.

Rhysa shrugged and rifled through the stack. She lifted an oil painting of a snow-laden scene. "This is beautiful. It reminds me of my homeland."

Emily peeked at the back and gave a small gasp. The painting was signed by Lainy then said, "to Rhysa."

Rhysa flipped it over. She looked up with narrowed eyes. "Why didn't she give this to me?"

"Perhaps she wasn't finished." Emily had no idea Lainy could paint, let alone be thoughtful enough to create something for her daughter. "What's the date say?"

Rhysa read it to herself. "This was painted after I first left. Between my sponsorship and my adoption."

Lainy did have a heart after all. Then what happened to change her?

Tears formed in Rhysa's eyes as she stared at the artwork. "I wish I was pretty and small. Then maybe she'd like me."

Though she possessed a strong build and height, Rhysa wasn't overweight. Emily shook her head. "Size isn't as important as you think. There's more at stake here."

"She's embarrassed to be seen with me and wants me to change."

Emily's lashes flickered. She had to keep her emotions in check. "Did she say that?"

Rhysa turned and ran up the stairs with the painting clutched in her fist. The pounding of her feet faded onto the next level of stairs before ending with the muffled slam of a door.

Emily dropped to her knees. "God, this child is hurting and I don't know how to stop the pain." Possible scenarios of the events at Lainy's house tangled themselves in Emily's prayer. Had Lainy actually said the words to Rhysa or were they only assumptions?

"God, don't allow Lainy's heart to be so cruel. Surround her with Your spirit. Put a yearning inside her to want to be their mother. And pour Your peace between Lainy and Robert."

Upstairs, between choruses of an electric guitar, a hard-metal vocalist screamed from speakers in Rhysa's room. Emily resisted the urge to stomp upstairs and instead strained to make out the chaotic chorus. When nothing emerged from the noise other than a throbbing ache in her forehead, she joined Dillon and Jabali by the pool.

Dillon climbed onto the deck. Water dripped from his body making a puddle on the concrete. "Is that thumping coming from Rhysa?"

Emily nodded. By the hard set of Dillon's jaw and the creases above his brow, Rhysa had set herself up for trouble. With water still dripping from his trunks, Dillon moved past Emily to the door.

Jabali, sprawled over an inner tube with his mask and snorkel pushed back on his head, clicked his tongue. "Rhysa knows not to play that station."

Relief eased some of the tension from Emily's muscles. At least the child hadn't been allowed to own the music.

The thumping came to a sudden halt, as did the hum of the outside air conditioner unit and the pool pump. Dillon had thrown the main breaker.

Emily expected the sudden silence to burst with angry voices. Instead, Dillon rejoined them by the pool. He settled into a lounge chair and patted the one beside him for Emily.

"Did you talk to her?" Emily eased onto the striped cushion.

"No." He took a long drink from a bottle of water on the table. "Rhysa needs time and space, not a lecture. But that doesn't mean she gets to break the rules."

He stared at the shop as a muscle in his jaw flexed. "I've not shown enough interest in either child to expect an audience. But that'll change."

Jabali paddled toward them. He hooked his feet on the side of the pool and fumbled with his snorkel, popping it in and out of his mouth. "Mom only wanted to play with Rhysa's hair."

Emily straightened. Dillon tensed beside her. Would they finally learn what happened to cause the discord between mother and daughter?

"What did you do over there today?" Emily probed for more information.

"Mom took us shopping. She bought us clothes to keep at her house. But she and Rhysa argued."

"Did things get better when you returned to the apartment?"

Jabali shrugged his bony shoulders. "Mom was trying to be nice."

"Would you want to go back?" Dillon rubbed his scarred shoulder. Emily knew the situation stressed him.

"Yeah, if Rhysa does. Mom's lonely."

Emily turned and met Dillon's frown. Something didn't add up. Lainy had to be keeping company with someone to explain the call Rhysa overheard. How could she be lonely?

Chapter Ten

A few weeks later …

Dillon stood and stretched to work out the kinks along his spine. Anxious to finish the surprises, he'd worked straight through breakfast and lunch.

He glanced at his phone hoping for an excuse to take a prolonged break, but the screen didn't register a call. Despite the risk, Robert refused to leave the cabin. He was determined to stay put, stating he wouldn't keep running.

Situated far off the beaten path, the cabin was hard to find and provided an easy lookout. For someone who hadn't been there before, it was next to impossible to find. Dillon scratched his chin as he considered those who did know of its location. Hadn't Robert taken some businessmen there for a retreat a few years ago? And, of course, Lainy knew of the property.

Lainy. She'd been quiet since the children's short visit. But the rent would come due at the end of the month, meaning he'd hear from her soon, unless he transferred money ahead of time. Dillon sighed. He didn't like carrying the decisions of the family. If he didn't send the money, not only would she call, she might ask to see the kids again. He'd talk it over with

Emily. She had a good sense of what to do in situations like this.

He'd grown too dependent on the kids' nanny, relying on her friendship more than he did his brother's. Despite the small voice warning him to back off, he smiled every time he thought of her, often over little memories like last night.

"My folks would like to meet the kids. They say when I'm home, I talk about the two nonstop. Would you mind if we took a day trip to the farm Thursday?"

"Please!" Rhysa and Jabali both begged.

How could he refuse? He hadn't seen Rhysa excited about anything since meeting her father at the game. A small part of him felt left out. But work would keep him tied to the shop. "Sure. Sounds fun."

Emily had reached for the lemonade after his approval. Jabali, still excited, jumped and clapped, knocking Emily's arm that held the pitcher. Sweet, yellow liquid lurched from the open container, splashing over her plate of uneaten food and soaking her denim jeans. Dillon could still hear her laughter mingled with giggles from the children.

His stomach rumbled, interrupting his musings. He should've stopped for lunch. Now Maurita would have everything cleaned up and there was nothing to eat in his cottage.

The shop door opened. He looked up to see Emily breeze through. "Hope you're hungry. I come bearing lunch." She braced a hip against the worktable and slid a plate laden with chips and a sandwich in his direction.

Dillon glanced from the Rueben, one of his favorites, then back to the woman who kept stealing his thoughts. "Thanks."

"Don't thank me, thank Maurita. She made it and insisted I bring it to you since you've been too busy to join us." Her eyes left Dillon's and searched the shop for his latest project. Good for his ego, she always showed interest in his work.

Even his favorite sandwich couldn't pull him away from a chance to impress the strawberry blonde. "Come on. If you can keep a secret, I'll share what I've been working on."

A wide smile lit her features. With an excuse to touch her, he guided her toward the back of the shop. Tall for a woman, they made a good match. Dillon didn't have to strain down to meet her eyes ... or if he ever worked up the nerve ... her lips.

Emily moved to a side bench and gasped. "This is beautiful."

"Just wait, it gets better." He stretched the ceiling fixture's cord to the nearest outlet. His latest design burst to life with a colorful bouquet of bubbles.

"Oh!" Emily threw her hands to her face. "Dillon! You create the most beautiful things."

The awe in her voice swelled his chest. He smiled as he considered what her reaction would be when she learned it was for Rhysa. Dillon scooted beside Emily and reached for her hand. He moved their fingers to the handmade polyester bubbles. "Since you're definitely not a child, you can touch it."

The teasing phrase took him back to their first introduction.

She turned and searched his eyes.

Dillon soaked in her crystal gaze and kept his hand over hers. Without risking his heart too far, he wanted to convey a part of what he felt. If for nothing else, to know if Emily's heart was tempted, too.

Too soon, sadness shadowed her blue eyes and she broke contact. Emily cleared her throat and moved her hand along the coiled spines connecting the bulbs.

The farther her fingers trailed from his, the deeper the ache pulled in his chest. He was losing against a group of people he knew nothing about. He couldn't follow Emily to the mission field. His livelihood was here. Surely God wouldn't call him away from the children—not when they needed him most?

"Who is this for?"

Pulling himself from conflicting thoughts, he answered, "Rhysa. The girl needs color in her room." He turned to the table beside them. "And this one's for Jabali, our little baseball coach."

Emily's brow furrowed as she met his then dropped to the fixture. Didn't she consider Jabali hers, too? Nanny or not, the children loved her, and Dillon was sure Emily returned the feeling.

"You're so thoughtful." Her wistful voice made him wish he'd also prepared one for her. Her fingers ran along the black powder-coated metal. She traced the cutout batter and trailed the ball to the pitcher then around to the catcher where the batter slid safely home. "A home run."

Too bad Dillon was striking out.

Desiring more of her time, he blurted out the first thought in his head. "Why haven't you married?" He inwardly groaned. Not the best pick of conversation topics.

A smile crept into the corner of her mouth. "I suppose the same reason you haven't."

"Touché." He scratched the tip of his chin. Their friendly jarring of recent should've prepared him for her quick response. "But I haven't had the best examples for encouragement."

Emily's eyes narrowed. What had he started? He could feel the bean ball aimed straight for him before it was thrown.

"I could understand that with Robert and Lainy's marriage, but weren't your parents a nice example?"

He felt his defense build. "Sure. But Mom died, and look what's left of Dad."

She shook her head in disapproval. "Do you think your dad would change any of it if he could? Because I imagine the years he had with your mother, and the sons that came as a blessing of that union, are worth it all to him."

Of course her logic made sense, to one who'd probably never dealt with a broken heart. But he had—twice. And if he wasn't careful, this charming third time might have him rooming with his dad.

Dillon didn't mean for the conversation to be on him. He pointed a finger at Emily. "You still haven't given me your reason."

She tossed her hair and shrugged. "No one ever asked."

***

Emily tried to hide the longing in her voice. What had happened? Until accepting the nanny position, she'd been perfectly content with her life. Missionary work had been challenging, or so she'd thought. Though in retrospect, none of her experiences could compare to the challenge brought on by the Brewingtons. Leaving them would pose the biggest hurdle she'd faced yet.

From the corner of her eye, she caught Dillon rubbing his scarred shoulder. "Does it hurt?"

"Sometimes."

"You always seem bothered by it when I'm around."
Not a good sign. Her heart plummeted. She fought to
stay focused on Dillon and not give in to her emotions.

Like the evening shadow settling over a forest of
trees, his hazel eyes darkened "Do you ever see
yourself doing something other than missionary work?"
A meditative hush crowded out the teasing atmosphere.

Emily stared at her sandaled feet and stammered, "I
… I don't know." She put a few steps between her and
Dillon as though interested in the tools scattered on the
table. "I'm just trying to follow where I'm led to go."

"How do you know God's telling you to go there?"

The accusing tone in Dillon's voice was out of
character. He didn't need to get upset, after all, they
were just friends. New friends at that. Emily cleared her
throat. How could she explain the workings of the
Spirit?

"If I try to do something other than what the Spirit's
leading me to do, I feel restless and doubtful of my
decision. But when I align myself where I feel He's
calling me then I'm at peace." A sigh relaxed her. She
was able to say exactly what she felt. *Thank you, God.*

Dillon's slow nod was followed by an intense
scrutiny in his eyes. "So … you have complete peace
about this next trip?"

She tensed all over again. With a sigh, she
straightened her back and pushed past him. "Like I said
before, some things are still fuzzy, but the details will
work out in time."

"Let's hope they do. Kurdistan's a long way from
home to find out you were wrong."

***

Emily left Dillon to eat alone. What caused his mood to foul? If she allowed herself to hope, she'd think he was growing fond of her. But that couldn't happen. She had no idea how long she'd be gone once leaving the states, and she couldn't expect him to wait. And why had she answered his question about marriage with, "No one ever asked.?"

Her stomach soured with disgust. "I'm not so desperate I'd marry anyone who asked." Hopefully Dillon hadn't interpreted it that way.

She squinted at the sunburst sky. "God, keep me focused on Your will and not worry about things I can't change."

Rhysa stood at the corner of the house.

Emily fanned her blouse as she strolled across the yard to meet her. "What are you doing?" Rhysa didn't like the hot weather, and was usually in the pool, if outside at all.

"I saw him from my window." The girl's face beamed as she pointed toward a flowerbed beside the shop. "Look. Is that our rabbit?"

Contently grazing, a rabbit sat with one ear up and the other down. "Let's get a closer look."

They edged nearer, slowly weaving around another mound of landscaping. The ear that hung showed a tear in the lobe and signs of recent healing.

Rhysa smiled. "That's him. That's who I've been praying for!"

Emily reached for Rhysa's palm and held it open. Although faded, traces of blue ink still showed, but the word *bunny* was now in Rhysa's handwriting.

"And like that bunny your name is written on Jesus' hands. But instead of ink, they are nail scars." She smiled into Rhysa's eyes. "God sees you as someone worth dying for. He could never forget you."

Rhysa chewed her bottom lip. "Maybe you're right." She scuffed the grass with her bare toe. "But what do I do when it feels like He has?"

Emily pictured her prayer journal and many others that she'd filled over the years. "Write out a prayer to God. Ask Him to protect you from doubt—because that's the enemy working against you. And ask God to open your eyes to the way He's showing you He cares. Then you'll not only see His love, you'll feel it, too."

"Is that what you do when you're far from home?"

"That's what I do no matter where I am. I always want to feel God's love and understand how He's working in my life."

She turned back to the rabbit. "Then I will name him, *Pam'yatala.*"

Emily raised a brow. She recognized the word as Ukrainian. "What does it mean?"

"Remembered."

They each returned to the house and found Jabali on the kitchen phone. Maurita smiled warmly and nodded her head in enthusiasm. "Mrs. Brewington called."

A sudden knot hardened Emily's stomach but was probably nothing to the way Rhysa felt. Jabali gave a tentative smile toward his sister then held the phone toward her. "Mom wants to talk to you."

She rolled her eyes before adjusting the receiver to her ear.

The doorbell rang keeping Emily from overhearing the conversation. *Help her feel You near, God.* The short prayer was all she could offer.

Emily swung the door open. A man in a dark navy suit leaned forward as if to enter. Emily stuck her foot out to block his path. "And you are who?"

He smiled warmly. "I'm Mark Redfield. A friend of the family." He playfully blocked the doorway as if she might try to exit. "And who are you?"

Emily relaxed and introduced herself. "The Brewingtons' nanny.

"Ah yes, we've spoken before." He entered as she stepped to the side.

Jabali waved from the kitchen. "Hi, Mark. Want to go swimming with me?"

Mark started to chuckle and shake his head, but a sneeze attacked him. "Ah. Excuse me." He sniffed and cleared his throat. "Someone must have cleaned with bleach. It always makes me sneeze."

"Guess what?" Jabali perched forward with excitement. "We're going to Emily's farm tomorrow!"

"That's nice, but I'm here to talk to your dad."

This made the second time Mark brushed Jabali off. Emily bristled. She realized not everyone was a fan of children, but that didn't excuse rude behavior.

"Dad's not here. But mom's on the phone with Rhysa."

Mark's forehead furrowed as he swung toward Rhysa. "Why is she calling?" The question came out mumbled more from thought than conversation.

"Duh. Because she's our mother?" Rhysa turned her back to the man.

Emily sighed. Rhysa shouldn't be rude either. She motioned Mark to the door. "Why don't you talk to Dillon?"

Mark tapped his fingers against the briefcase he carried. "How about I talk to you first? Could we go into the office for privacy?"

"No." For whatever reason, she didn't want to tell him it was locked. "But we can talk in the sitting room."

Once seated, Mark leaned forward with his elbows on his knees. He brought his hands together under his chin. "I'm worried about Robert. I've not been able to get a hold of him."

"Then why talk to me? Why not Dillon?"

"I'm will talk to him, but I wanted to know how the family was doing first. How are the kids behaving without Lainy?"

Emily's back stiffened. He seemed like a nice guy, but having never met him before his questioning made her uncomfortable. "They're doing well enough."

"Good." He let one hand drop and raked the other through the side of his hair. "I'm not just Robert's friend, I'm also his marketer, so you can see why I need to speak to him."

Emily nodded, not understanding why he'd involved her in conversation. Though it might just be her perception, but his questions didn't seem to line up.

Rhysa stormed past them to the stairs. She glanced back long enough to glare at Mark—the family friend?

Chapter Eleven

"Hey, Mark." Dillon looked up from his drawing as his family's long-time friend entered the shop. "You're looking tan. Been fishing?"

"I've taken the boat out a few times."

"Still have the Cobalt Bowrider?" Though it had been a while since Dillon accompanied Mark fishing, he knew the boat was engineered to perfection. The sleek, blue, fiberglass hull never went unnoticed when on the water.

"Yeah, but not for long. I plan to upgrade I've got my eye on a cruiser. She's a real beauty with twin-engines that run like a Ferrari." Mark's eyes squinted as he looked into the distance. "You know what they say, 'Begin where you like. End where you belong.'"

Dillon clicked his tongue. "Sounds like it'll set you back quite a bit."

Mark's eyes penetrated Dillon's for a brief moment before relaxing with a smile. "Anything new happening?"

Dillon accepted the quick topic change as Mark often jumped from one item of interest to another. "I've been swimming with the kids. Watched the new monster flick with them—"

"You? The recluse!" Mark's smile broadened. "Couldn't have anything to do with the new hired help could it?"

Dillon refused to let the thoughtless phrase bother him. Emily wasn't just hired help—the family needed her. "She's a nice person and a good friend. The kids are doing really well under her care."

"Good. Get married and you both can adopt them. They'd probably do better with you two."

Another careless comment. Dillon shook his head and moved to the window. Mark too often spoke without thought. "We've been having problems with coyotes coming too close."

Mark joined him staring intently out the window. "I've heard of a recent attack further west of here. Not very safe for the kids."

Dillon crossed his arms in front of his chest and faced him. "We wouldn't have a problem if they weren't baited. It's almost as if someone wanted to scare us off."

Mark scratched his head and turned to the back of the shop where Dillon kept his finished work. "You have some weird neighbors."

He moved before Dillon could read his expression.

What was Dillon concerned about anyway? The company marketer wasn't anyone to worry about. He needed the business to grow as much as they did. Especially with his expensive taste in toys. "I'm not worried. I'll catch whoever it is on camera soon enough."

The security company had installed four outdoor cameras after reprogramming the security system on the house. Either a neighbor had tossed the food hoping to keep their own property clean and didn't want to admit it, or his spoken suspicion was true. Someone wanted them gone.

Mark glanced around the shop. "Your kind of talent is hard to find."

"That's because it's hard to support. Without the success of the business, I'd never afford half of the material I work with." He waved for him to follow. "Take a look at Rhysa's new light. This polyester didn't come cheap."

Mark blew a low whistle. "Promise me, if anything ever happens to your brother, you'll keep designing."

The hair on the back of Dillon's neck stood on end. How much did Mark know? Had Robert confided in him?

Mark moved to a copper lamp with resin crystal snowflakes. "And here's the Tuscany lamp Robert told me about. I know exactly where to send him with this. He mentioned he was going to take some time off, but I figured he'd be back by now." Mark rotated the lamp on its base and took in every angle. "Must be nice having enough money and not have to work all the time."

"What is it with you and money?" Dillon's patience grew thin. "I told him to take all the time he needed. We're doing fine here."

"I guess he went to the cabin?"

Dillon jerked his head toward their inquisitive friend. "Do you need him for anything?"

"Yeah. When you talk to him next, tell him to answer my calls. I can't help grow his business without him."

Dillon watched him leave by the lane looping around the side of the house. Were his frayed nerves because he didn't trust anyone at the moment or was there more to Mark's visit?

***

The next morning Dillon leaned against the counter listening as Maurita reprimanded him for skipping meals. Her fast chatter faded to the back of his mind when Emily waltzed through the door wearing jeans cut off below the knee and a white T-shirt tied at the hip.

His self-imposed deadline no longer seemed important. *Ask me to go with you, Emily.*

"Good morning."

The darkest cloud could brighten with her smile.

"Does your presence at the table mean you're done with the surprises?"

"Yep. I put the finish coat on Jabali's last night. They're now ready for presentation."

"Are you going to give them to the kids this morning or wait until we get home tonight?"

"About that. Maybe I should drive all of you down. I wouldn't want you to risk having car problems."

An instant frown covered her mouth. "My car runs fine. You should stop worrying and focus on finishing your orders."

"I don't really have an order. Just another prototype a company can decide if they want or not."

"Still, we'll be fine." She caught him staring. "What are you looking at?" She swiped a finger over the bridge of her nose.

"Your freckles."

Her chin came up a notch. "I don't have freckles. They're angel kisses."

With a finger to her jaw, Dillon turned her face to his. "Then judging by the dusting on your nose, that angel must have really liked you."

A pink glow highlighted her cheeks and caused a strange flutter in his chest. He took a deep breath and held her smiling gaze. Too soon the children entered with excitement over their trip, interrupting the playful banter.

Dillon forced a smile past his self-pity. Engulfed in their plans, they didn't realize how much he wanted to be a part of them.

An hour later he waved good-bye as the old sedan pulled out of the garage. The oil and water had checked out okay, despite the ugly stain left on the garage floor. He applied a cleanser to the floor to soak up the spill.

Something rattled on a shelf. *Odd.* He replaced the cleanser and put in a fruitless half-hearted search before starting his next project—installing the children's new lighting. His other projects could wait.

In the shop, he retrieved Jabali's light first. It would be the easiest as it was less fragile. Before he could make it out the door his phone rang. "Hello."

"Dillon, it's Lainy."

He clenched his jaw, wishing he didn't have to deal with her, and waited for his sister-in-law to continue.

"I talked to the kids this week, and since Rhysa doesn't want to come to the apartment again I've decided to stop by on Sunday."

Dillon set the lamp down and crossed an arm over his chest supporting his elbow. "That's a busy day for us. We attend morning services and then visit my dad."

"I'm well aware of that." Her response sounded agitated. "I lived by you long enough to realize you're a creature of habit. I didn't plan on showing until late afternoon."

If he was a creature of habit, could the same be said for his brother? If so, no wonder he'd been easy to track. Not wanting to agree, but realizing there wasn't much he could do to stop her, Dillon sighed and paced the floor. "Fine. But why now? Why start caring—or is it the rent check you need?"

"That stings, Dillon, but I wouldn't expect you to understand. You stay hidden in your shop, oblivious to what's happening in the house full of strangers. It could've housed a family, but a vital part was always missing—your brother."

Dillon slipped the phone back in his pocket after Lainy disconnected. Though he didn't want to admit the fact, there was more supporting Lainy's move than money. Robert wasn't the same type of husband their dad had been. Their father was home almost every evening. And if he had to be away, he often took the family with him. Robert never did.

Robert loved his family. Still loved his wife. But the facts had yet to slap him in the face. They needed more of him. He needed less of the business. Dillon sighed. *God, it's time for a blunt heart-to-heart with my brother. Prepare him for what he needs to hear and give me the words I need to speak.*

Dillon brought Jabali's light to the kid's room. Maurita stepped out from cleaning the bathroom and clapped her hands. "Good. Good! He'll like very much."

Her English was improving, thanks to Emily.

As he finished twisting the last wires together, his phone rang again. Dillon ignored it until he finished securing the light to the wall. He still had another light to install. The interruptions were setting him back.

He climbed from the ladder and called from the top of the stairs. "Okay, flip that breaker I showed you."

"*Si, Senor* Dillon."

He could hear Maurita's footsteps clip across the tiled floor toward the garage. Dillon reached for his phone to check who'd called when a shriek sounded from the cook.

He raced down the stairs, jumping the last three. Within seconds he stood at the doorway with Maurita. A rat scurried along a shelf.

Rats? They'd never had a problem with rodents.

A bucket toppled over. Another rat scurried up the stairs before Dillon could slam the door. The rodent ran past their feet and into the house.

Maurita squealed and danced in place.

Dillon grabbed a broom to hunt for the uninvited pest. "Don't worry, I'll find him."

Sweat beaded across the cook's forehead while her hands waved the air. A rapid string of Spanish rolled off her tongue. She wouldn't be easy to calm.

"You go home. I'll call an exterminator."

Maurita continued to rant as she grabbed her purse and headed for the front door.

Dillon sighed. He'd never find the rat on his own. He flipped through the phone book and glanced over the list of exterminators. Never having needed their services before, he had no idea how to choose one. Deciding on the business with the biggest ad, he grabbed his phone.

On the front of the screen, beneath missed call, read Emily's name. He called her first.

"Dillon, I'm glad you got the call."

"Are you all right?" A small dose of panic tightened his muscles.

"Oh yes. But for whatever reason, my car started acting funny. I'm pulling in at …"

Dillon listened to her directions. "I'll attach the trailer and be right there."

First rats, now this? He made the call to take care of the rodents then turned off the alarm and hid the key for the exterminator.

***

Emily pressed the pedal to the floorboard and leaned forward as if it would do any good. She couldn't push the car from behind the wheel and no amount of gas would help the knocking of the engine.

She turned at the nearest exit as the engine began to squeal. *This is bad.* She parked at a fast food restaurant as a white cloud of steam escaped around the hood.

"Whew, it's hot in here." Jabali waved his hand in front of his face.

Heat from the engine wafted through the open cowl vent. "Let's go inside and get something cool to drink while we wait for your uncle."

Her poor car. Emily paused at the chrome grill. The engine had definitely overheated. Why? She'd been careful to check the fluid before she left. *Sorry, Grandpa.*

"Come on, Emily, I'm thirsty." Rhysa waved from the door of the restaurant. "Can we get something to eat, too?"

After their order was filled, Emily weaved through tables full of road crews. A low catcall didn't go unnoticed, but she would never show the benefit of recognition. Was a whistle all they could think of, seriously?

Dillon would never stoop to that.

How did she know? She almost laughed out loud, defending Dillon to her own conscious. Still, she was certain he possessed more manners and ingenuity than a whistle required.

Her cheeks warmed at the memory of him staring at her freckles. If only he'd been the one to kiss them all in place.

"I wonder if any of them wanted to be baseball players."

Emily started. She cleared her throat and refocused. "Who are you talking about?" She gave Jabali an amused look and passed out their tacos, thankful her thoughts couldn't be read.

"All these men." He motioned around the room. "They work so hard outside. I bet they wish they were playing ball instead."

Rhysa shared an amused look with Emily. "He thinks he's going to play ball when he grows up."

"Dad and Mom both say I will."

The brightness in Rhysa's eyes dulled with the mention of her mother. She stopped eating and toyed with a packet of sauce. "Mom said she wanted to see us again. But I told her I didn't want to go."

Pain for Rhysa's turmoil squeezed Emily's heart. "I'm sorry. I wish you felt differently."

"Why?" Rhysa glared at Emily.

"What was it like when you first stayed with Robert and Lainy?"

Rhysa glanced away. "Fun, I guess."

"Could you speak English?"

"Yes. That was my fourth sponsorship in America."

Jabali spoke around his food. "She helped teach me."

"What I'm trying to say, is if things were good then, what changed for them to be bad now?"

"Mom left." As if Rhysa knew Emily wanted more, she heaved a sigh and continued. "She was always on her phone. Texting or talking to someone. She didn't have time for us anymore."

"And where was your dad?"

"Gone. Like he is now."

Though it wasn't good news, at least Emily had more direction for her prayers. The common scenario had hit a lot of homes with the increase in technology. Couldn't parents see how easily it tore down their families if not controlled?

Emily finished and rolled up her paper. A worker rose from a nearby table as the other occupants murmured encouragement. *Oh boy. Here we go.*

She glanced up and met milk chocolate eyes accented by sandy blonde hair. The handsome man cocked a charming grin and thumbed toward the empty seat across from her. "Mind if I set down."

"Actually I do. We're almost done."

An eyebrow rose on her admirer. With looks like his he probably didn't face rejection very often. He shifted his weight to one hip and hung a thumb off a belt loop. "If you're in a hurry, maybe we should just exchange phone numbers."

Emily tossed her long hair and leaned back against the seat. "Maybe. But first let me see if I understand you correctly. You saw me and the kids over here and suddenly thought you might want to get to know me better ..." she gave a playful grin, "because you're ready for fatherhood?"

His eyes stayed friendly as his smile broadened, undeterred by the challenge. "I'm already a dad. No big deal." He gave the kids a wink.

"Oh. So you make enough money you're interested in supporting more?" Emily emphasized the last word and almost snickered at his comical expression. The banter had been harmless and even fun, but if there was anyone she'd consider building a relationship with it was Dillon. She extended her hand. "I'm flattered by your interest, but I'm not available."

The man took pressed a light kiss to the top of her hand. "It's been fun."

Amused, Emily turned toward Rhysa after he rejoined his friends. Only then did she notice Dillon standing a few tables away.

Chapter Twelve

Dillon tried to wipe the frown from his face before reaching the table. A group of men jeered their friend as he rejoined them. How would Dillon have reacted if Emily had switched phone numbers with him? The thought did nothing to ease the tension stiffening his spine.

"Hello family." As Dillon took a seat with Emily and the kids, he threw a stern glance toward the table of admirers meant to say *I'm the reason she's not available*. No matter where she went, Emily's vibrant personality and beauty attracted attention.

"You made good time." Emily offered him the extra soda sitting in the tray. "I got this for you. The kids said it's what you drink."

He took a sip to show his appreciation. "Thanks."

She kept her eyes diverted, as if embarrassed by the attention he'd witnessed.

Vibrant, beautiful, confident, great sense of humor, and now humbleness. The list of Emily's admirable qualities grew faster than his heart could keep up.

"If all of you are done, let's take a look at the car." He rose and pulled out Rhysa's chair while waiting for Jabali and Emily to scoot off the adjacent bench seat.

Rhysa slipped her hand into his as they approached the parking lot. Just like she would do with her dad. Dillon's chest swelled with gratitude. *Thank you, God, for helping me see what I'd been missing.*

Lainy's words from earlier rang back in truth, "… *Hidden in your shop, oblivious to what's happening in the house full of strangers …*"

He released Rhysa's hand and pulled her to him in a sideways hug. "Let's get the car running so I can drive it home and you guys can take my truck."

Rhysa stiffened. Not the response he'd expected. She'd been excited to go to the farm. She turned her face toward him. Her brow furrowed. "What about who was following us?"

"What?" Dillon glanced from Rhysa to Emily. "Someone was following you?"

"I thought he was just riding my bumper." Emily's eyes were wide with innocence as she switched to Rhysa. "He didn't turn in here when we did."

"What type of vehicle was it?" His question went unanswered. "Did you get the license plate number?"

"I didn't think—"

Rhysa interrupted Emily. "She was busy praying for the driver."

Emily nodded. "I didn't want his driving to get someone hurt. But I kept my eyes opened!"

Although her comment was meant to lighten the seriousness of the situation, a headache started to pound in Dillon's forehead. He swept the parking lot for anyone watching. "Let's check your car." What was happening to their secure suburban life?

He raised the heavy hood. "Did you check the oil and water?"

"No. It was too hot." Emily met him with a shop towel as he removed the dipstick.

"We won't need that. It's dry as a bone."

"What—No! We checked it before we left." Traces of panic laced her words. The car held a lot of sentiment for her.

"Jabali, get me the flashlight from my truck, would you?"

Like a field mouse busily gathering grain, Jabali scurried to the truck to do as asked. The boy always seemed excited to pitch in. If their farm trip was canceled, as Dillon expected it would be, he'd have the boy helping him in the shop once they were home.

"Here you go." Jabali dropped the light into Dillon's hand as he reached out from beneath the car.

"I see your problem." He blew a sigh between gritted teeth. Someone had drilled a tiny hole in the tank. Nothing that would show much when sitting in the garage but definitely affect the performance once the oil heated.

Dillon slid out from beneath the vehicle and stood to brush himself off. Did he discuss what he'd found in front of the children or make them stay in the truck? One look at Rhysa gave him the answer. He'd seen, firsthand, the damage done by withholding the truth about his injury. As family, they had a right to know.

"Was anyone in the garage yesterday?" He explained the rats, then the hole in the oil tank. The solemn faces of his small audience were quiet with thought.

Rhysa muttered, "It was probably Mark."

Dillon caught the phrase. "What do you have against Mark?" Although he'd developed his own doubts toward their marketer, he needed more reason to understand them.

A small gasp escaped Emily. "It may be nothing, but while in the kitchen, I did open the door to the garage to show him my car. But we didn't step in. He'd only wanted to look."

"How did he know about your car?" Dillon rubbed his shoulder.

"I figured you or Robert had told him."

After mounting the Plymouth onto the trailer, Dillon crossed the highway to return home. He was sorry to disappoint the kids, but the old sedan wouldn't see anyone to the farm until it was fixed.

His phone rang. "Robert?"

"Just wanted to give you an update. I did eventually leave the cabin after what you said about someone asking dad, and it's a good thing. I went back today to get a few things and surprised a shooter."

Dillon's blood went cold. "Were you shot?" The air in the cab grew thin as Emily and the kids overheard his comment.

"Slight nick in the arm and I have to replace a side window in my car." The rest of Robert's description blurred under the fact Dillon's brother had again, nearly met his fate.

"Hole up somewhere new. Get a spot with room service and don't move until you hear from me. I have an idea who's responsible. I'll let you know as soon as I can."

One glance at the cab's occupants and Dillon knew they expected an explanation.

***

Dillon stopped in front of the house instead of driving around back. The muscles along his spine tightened, something wasn't right. "Everyone stay put until I check things out."

"Why?" The children's combined voices belied their concern.

Emily turned toward them. "Let your uncle make sure the rats are gone. If there're any left, we wouldn't want to let more into the house."

You're an angel. He resisted the urge to touch her hand and slid from the truck. The key had been replaced where he left it for the exterminator. He slipped it into the lock to make certain it hadn't been switched. The door unlocked with ease and swung open against the wall. Dillon stepped inside.

The office door stood open. The frame by the knob splintered from force. Anger overrode all fear as he made his way through the sitting room to Robert's desk. The computer had been turned on though it appeared the intruder hadn't succeeded in breaking into their system. Careful not to touch anything, Dillon backed out of the room and called the police as he checked the rest of the house.

By the time the officers had come and gone, they still didn't have any answers. The police were unable to locate any fingerprints and the utility source to the cameras had been cut. Another dead end.

Dillon unlocked the desk drawer to insure nothing had been disturbed. A sigh of relief relaxed his shoulders. The passwords were still there.

Emily appeared in the doorway. "The kids are in bed, though I doubt they'll fall asleep any time soon."

She covered a yawn with her hand. "Jabali's light looks great. Rhysa can't wait to see hers tomorrow."

"Yeah, at least there was one bright spot in their day." He rounded the desk to stand beside her. She'd pulled her hair into a high ponytail, giving her a youthful look.

"So why aren't you available?" Her furrowed brow reminded him he'd thrown the question from left field. "That's what you told your admirer at the restaurant."

Emily tilted her head to the side. "You know I'm leaving." Her gaze fell to the floor. "Besides, I knew he wasn't serious."

"No, I'd have to disagree. I think he was definitely attracted to you. In fact, you probably could've had your choice of any of the men at the table."

"Thanks for your vote of confidence." Her lips pursed as she controlled a smile. "But I meant he wasn't serious about a relationship."

Dillon's gaze swept from her eyes to her hair and ended on her lips. "Don't you ever date just to see a movie or have dinner?"

She visibly swallowed. "No. Does that make me weird?" Her eyebrows rose in nervous anticipation. His opinion mattered.

"Just more interesting."

She seemed to take his response into consideration. "When I was a teen, I heard a visiting youth pastor tell us that type of dating was practice for divorce. Instead, we should wait to spend time with someone when both individuals are thinking of marriage."

A fierce pounding drummed inside his chest. *Do I make you think of marriage?* He searched her eyes, not sure what to say but wanting to know her thoughts.

He finally settled on asking about her family, anything to keep her talking. "Did your sister and brothers adhere to the same rule?"

"Not exactly. My parents didn't enforce the rule, just encouraged common sense then trusted us to apply it in our own lives."

Dillon nodded. "Sounds like it was a wise decision and probably saved you from unnecessary heartache."

"But you weren't saved from it, were you?" Her blue eyes pierced through to his heart.

The need to blink and break eye contact had him staring at the desk. "No, I wasn't. But I also wasn't as logical as you in my approach."

"I knew there had to be a reason."

"A reason for what?" She had his attention now.

"That you weren't married." Her voice softened. "You're a great catch. The only reason a man like you isn't married has to be because of a broken heart or he's playing for the wrong side of the team."

A rumble burst from his chest. "The wrong side of—I won't even venture what you mean by that, though I have an idea."

Her humor eased Dillon from the growing discomfort of having been read so easily. As the humorous moment calmed, his eyes settled on her bright smile, warming his thoughts. If she hadn't dated like most people did, had she ever been kissed?

Emily cleared her throat and glanced at the other room. "How did someone get to my car?"

He swallowed disappointment. The thought wasn't going to go away without closure. Eventually, they'd both have to address the building attraction between them.

Dillon scratched his jaw and said, "I don't know. If it was Mark, maybe he waited until he thought I wouldn't be looking and came back around the house. He could have slipped in through the door to the garage."

"Rhysa doesn't seem to like him. Has she mentioned why?"

Dillon shook his head. "Whatever and whoever, it's now personal. All of you could have been seriously hurt."

"All it did—"

"Could have caused an accident on the interstate. Whoever's behind this is careless, isn't concerned who is hurt, and definitely wants Robert dead."

***

Emily wiped down the counter and stove after Dillon said goodnight. The only thing wrong with bacon sandwiches was the cleanup. She squeezed her sponge in the sink full of hot soapy water before removing the burner dials to clean underneath. Maurita kept a spotless kitchen. Emily didn't want her returning to a mess. Although Dillon voiced his concern she might not come back for a while, Emily didn't agree. Maurita had seen the children disappointed too many times to add to their heartache.

She covered the skillet to save the grease for gravy in the morning. Though healthier if made from oil, the rare treat wouldn't hurt. Without thinking she slid a hand over her hip.

Sometimes she missed being abroad. While away serving, she'd been protected from the constant push to have a fit and sculpted body. Not that anyone around her had commented, but every other billboard, magazine ad, or commercial seemed to have an opinion of what she should look like. And each morning the mirror in her bedroom acknowledged she didn't make the cut.

A Christian's esteem wasn't supposed to be based on their own image, but the image of the God who created them and died for them. And if Emily lost sight of that, watchful Rhysa would too. *God, help me to remember I'm not of this world. Protect me from its entrapping lies.* Peace fell across her shoulders like a light mist. Emily was accustomed to the quick response to prayer. The spiritual battle that constantly fought control for her soul had been made aware to her at an early age.

She'd been nine years old the summer she'd gone away to camp for the first time. Every sermon preached had soaked into her with crystal clarity. Especially the sermon centered on Ephesians 6:12, *"For we wrestle not against flesh and blood, but against principalities, against powers, against the rulers of the darkness of this world, against spiritual wickedness in high places."*

The next verses taught how to protect herself with the whole armor of God. Just like with the subject of dating, Emily had absorbed the logical wisdom and applied it.

She knelt beside the kitchen counter. *God, thank you for your protection today over us all. But the threat still remains. Shod our feet and guide us from harm. Open our eyes to what we can't see and shield Robert from the devil's fiery darts.*

Emily remained on her knees, patiently waiting on the Spirit. Through the silence a nagging thought kept interrupting her concentration. Finally, the thought pushed its way to the surface. From earlier in the evening, the police officer's accusing voice returned, asking why Dillon hadn't been targeted.

Dillon? Her natural reaction wanted to defend him. He couldn't be responsible for the threats. Aside from the fact he was home with them most of the time, Emily knew in her heart he was trustworthy. She wouldn't fall for the enemy's distraction.

God, show me how to turn this to good. After a few minutes, she turned to sit and lean against the cabinet, relieving the pressure on her knees. Still, she sat in silence. Beginning to doze, Emily caught her head from falling to her shoulder. *Help me stay awake. I feel like we're close to understanding something big.*

What seemed like moments later, but proved to be several minutes, Emily again caught herself falling asleep. She jerked her head up and the idea came to her. Why hadn't Dillon been targeted? The answer lay hidden inside the question.

Emily hurried through the back door and down the path. Had Dillon given thought to the same thing? Between the two of them, she was sure they'd understand more after they talked.

Focused on capturing elusive facts, Emily hadn't considered her safety. Her steps slowed as she sensed another's presence. Security lights illuminated the darkness, but only within their radius. To her left, like a thick blue gel, the pool cast a spooky glow.

Emily took a deep breath. Now wasn't the time to give into fear. She and Dillon were close to an answer. She knew it.

She jerked her attention forward, expecting to see someone standing in the path. Nothing. The silence of the evening thickened until all she heard was her own breathing. *Get moving, you dope. You're an open target standing in the light.*

The stone walkway beckoned her to safety. Emily started forward. Movement in the shadows brought her to a dead halt. She strained to see through the darkness.

The shadow moved.

Chapter Thirteen

Emily swallowed hard and edged toward the cottage. If she took off in a sprint, she'd beat whoever was waiting in the dark.

A coyote stepped into the light at the edge of the yard. She froze. Not what she'd expected. Running was no longer an ideal solution. The mangy animal continued to stare at her with an eerie focus.

Her skin prickled as her fear increased. *Don't panic. Remember what you've read.*

Before her mind could replay the facts, the coyote stretched his neck then tilted his nose, sniffing the air. Emily glanced at her shirt. She still wore the same clothes she'd cooked in. Like a Hawaiian luau, she'd presented herself as a stuffed pig.

"God, help me out of this one," she whispered. The wild canine took a tentative step forward. Emily maintained eye contact and matched his movement. She was sure he'd back away as long as she didn't show fear.

The coyote looked to his side before another of his pack trotted into the light. Like before, it too sniffed the air.

Dread weighed her down. She could scream for Dillon but didn't want to risk waking the children. One of them running outside with the coyotes was the last thing that needed to happen.

A hiss and yowl sounded from the dark. Both dogs looked to the side and up. Jumping against the fence, they yipped and whined at what could only be Shop Cat. "Thank you, Jesus!" Emily saw her chance and raced toward the cottage.

The door swung open before she had a chance to slow. Dillon stepped outside as she ran straight into his chest. Both arms encircled her waist and kept her from falling backward.

"Emily—what's wrong?" He glanced behind her toward the house.

She fought to maintain control even though it would be so easy to fall apart in the safety of his arms. "Coyotes—"

Dillon pulled back as he urged her inside then stepped toward the path. "Get out of here!" He waved his arms over his head as he growled out the command.

From the window, Emily saw the ends of their tails as they turned and disappeared into the darkened field. Something scurried across the yard. Within moments, Shop Cat bounded inside and onto the small couch.

The door shut, and Dillon reached for the frightened animal. "Maybe next time you'll think twice before staying out so late."

Emily moved beside them and stroked the cat's head. "He was an answer to prayer. Both coyotes smelled the bacon on my clothes and were a bit too curious. But this furry hero distracted them for me."

She bent her head toward the cat. "Didn't you?" Although stroking the soft animal's fur brought her comfort, the calming sensation was nothing compared to the nearness of Dillon.

"What were you doing out there?"

"Coming to talk to you."

His eyes held a mixture of concern and disapproval. "I do have a phone you know."

"I'll remember that for next time." She saw him glance out the window at the house and wanted to set his mind at ease. "The alarm's set. I'll punch in the code before I open the door."

Dillon shuffled the cat into her arms, his eyes more relaxed with the knowledge the children were safe. He stepped toward the mini kitchen. "How about a cup of coffee? But I'll be the one handling the cups in the microwave."

Emily took a seat in a wing-backed chair and smiled. "You don't feel like getting burned tonight?" She couldn't control the image of his bare chest teasing her mind.

Dillon's home, though much smaller than a bungalow, possessed similar warmth. Stained wooden chair railings and moldings accentuated the painted walls. Positioned on top of a bookcase was a framed photograph of what must have been Dillon with his brother and dad. Dillon had a bat swung over his shoulder while Robert wore a glove. Their dad stood between them with a proud smile.

Dillon returned a couple minutes later and glanced from her to the couch before setting the cups on the table. "You might be more comfortable over here." His eyes sparkled, enticing her to accept.

Her cheeks warmed at the invitation, but she still hadn't calmed from the threat outside. Her eyes dropped to Dillon's protective arms.

Yeah, distance was safest. Otherwise she might wind up snuggled against him, which is exactly where she'd like to be if only she weren't leaving.

Dillon interrupted her thoughts, "Is there anything wrong with sitting next to me?"

Emily blinked several times and looked down at the cat snuggled in her lap. Her throat tightened with unspoken emotion. *Please don't play with my heart.* Dillon didn't realize how little encouragement she needed. But they'd both be thankful later if they didn't move past friendship now.

"I came over to brainstorm with you." She lifted the cup to her lips. The warm, dark liquid calmed her frayed nerves. She took a sip before continuing. "Have you given thought to why the attacks haven't been against you?"

Dillon sighed and stretched his long legs out in front of him. "I think whoever it is wants the business."

"How would getting rid of Robert accomplish that?" She couldn't bring herself to say killing Robert, even though that's what the attacker had tried to do. On many occasions. "Wouldn't they have to get rid of you, too?" The idea made her cringe.

"I'm not an owner."

Emily stalled with her cup in the air. "Why not?" His family seemed so devoted to one another. She couldn't imagine their father choosing favorites.

"I didn't want to be." He motioned to the lamp beside them. "My talent lies in creating, not business. I didn't want the distraction."

Emily stared at him in admiration. "Or the money."

He simply shrugged. "What would I do with it? I have everything I want."

A muscle twitched in his jaw. "*Almost* everything." He pinned her with a challenging look. If she'd doubted it before, she couldn't deny the role she played in his want list now. He had made it all too clear.

Emily breathed a sigh of relief when he looked away. She hadn't risked her life with coyotes for this. They were supposed to focus on—Shop Cat stretched his paw, piercing her leg with his claws. "Ow!"

Dillon stood and scooped the cat from her lap. "You'll spoil him. He knows the crate's the only place he's allowed in the house.

Emily took another sip of coffee and stood. "I should leave anyway. We can brainstorm more tomorrow."

Dillon sighed. "Sure. I'll walk you to the door though."

That wasn't something Emily would argue about. But she hadn't expected him to hold her hand. Crazy sensations traveled up her arm and tangled her thoughts until the only thing she could do was feel.

Dillon shifted to look behind them. "Good, the mangy animals left."

Their absence was a blessing. Had they still been there, she wouldn't have been any help. Dillon's touch fogged her senses enough she'd forgotten everything but the man beside her.

They stopped at the door. Emily wished the path were longer. Instead of punching the code into the box, she stood staring at Dillon. He moved in closer. She could feel the heat of his body and smell the scent of his soap.

"You can stop me if you want."

Butterflies flitted inside her abdomen while everything else seemed numb. A smile enhanced his features before his mouth pressed against hers. Engulfed in the beauty of what was happening Emily closed her eyes. Her heart thumped an erratic beat. Was this love?

She drew back and gasped. "This can't happen."

Dillon stilled as a frown creased his brow. He didn't understand.

"I'll be leaving soon. To the other side of the world."

***

Emily kicked at the sheet twisted around her. Dillon's fallen expression kept repeating in her mind. Why didn't he say something? Didn't he understand?

Adding to her regrets was the fact she knew he'd been hurt in the past. Couldn't he see she was protecting him from that? Guilt sent a pang to her chest. Maybe she was just protecting herself.

Maybe? Ha. Who was she fooling? Not her and certainly not God.

But don't You see how detrimental this would be to our hearts? How can we build on something that distance will keep apart? Oh God, I'm so far out in left field. Have I completely fouled up? The family's use of baseball terms had even worked their way into her prayer life. When had they become such a strong part of her? Would she ever be able to separate herself from the Brewingtons?

***

Emily checked the mail Saturday afternoon. Rhysa said she had something in the stack. The girl had dropped the mail on the table and left the room. They'd had a good week together, but Emily supposed the idea of her mother's visit tomorrow weighed her down.

She saw the return address before seeing her name. The envelope would hold details of her trip to

143

Kurdistan. A corner of her mouth lifted. The tiny thrill was nothing in comparison to how she usually felt. With slow movements, she peeled open the flap.

Emily's summer had begun with building anticipation toward its end. Her next post wasn't far from the sea, something she'd experienced only once and always looked forward to again. Although recently, the memories that had often soothed her to sleep of gulls crying overhead and the lapping of the tide were replaced with thoughts of the children and Dillon.

Her heart ached, and she hadn't even left.

She slipped on her shoes intent on going for a walk. But where could she and feel safe? She looked for the children. A day in the park together would cure her blues.

At the shop, she watched from the door as Dillon showed Jabali how to hold the soldering gun at the right angle. Rhysa was bent over the worktable tracing a pattern onto stain glass.

"Wow, you've got some good workers today."

Rhysa stayed focused on her task. Jabali's smile didn't meet his eyes. What was wrong? A shiver of concern for Robert made her glance at Dillon.

"You guys continue what I've shown you. I'll be back." He motioned Emily back outside.

"What's wrong with them?" Emily twisted her hands. Aside from her nervousness over the children, she and Dillon still hadn't regained the comfort they'd shared with each other before the kiss.

His jaw flexed as he stared off to the side before speaking. "Why do you care?"

Dillon's gaze turned to her, though steady, he couldn't hide the hurt. "You'll be gone in a couple of months."

Emily swallowed hard. Self-pity, anger, resentment and sadness balled up inside her. "That's what I do. I work with children all around the world because I care."

"And what do you think you're accomplishing?"

His sudden disapproval cut through her like a knife. "We've talked about this. I organize the social work that enables orphanage workers and volunteers to interact and teach."

"But you leave. Just like you will here. What happens then?"

Her head began to ache. She searched for the constant smile in his eyes—it wasn't there. "I leave behind trained workers, Dillon."

"Not here, you won't. You're just setting them up for heartache."

"That hurts. And it's not true. They have you, and they'll have their dad back."

"Turn a blind eye if you want, but this is different, and you know it."

Dillon's words pinched her heart making it impossible to ignore the truth. Her eyes burned. She wanted to cry, but the fire that heated her veins kept her tears in check. "You don't have to be cruel just because I didn't let you keep kissing me. I did it to save your heart."

He moved as if to leave, but paused by her side. A sigh slipped past his lips before his eyes softened. "I wasn't referring to my heart," he tapped his chest, "but Rhysa and Jabali's."

Left standing alone, the weight of the world seemed to fall upon her. Her thoughts formed into a tangled knot. How could she make sense of what she no longer understood? She lifted her head as tears tracked down her cheeks. The field and stream offered the solitude she craved, but not at the risk of coyotes.

Emily returned to the house and stood in the doorway of the kitchen and garage. She stared at the oil stain left by her car. Without her Plymouth she had no way of escape.

Where could I go, but to the Lord ... a verse from an old hymn whispered comfort through her memories. She pulled the door closed and sat on the step in the garage. With her face cradled in her hands, she wept for all the pain in her heart. For the pain she'd undoubtedly cause the children and for the love she had to give up. Unable to pray, she knew the Holy Spirit would intercede for her and the Almighty Comforter would ease her aches.

Emily leaned back against the door and closed her eyes. The heated garage, though almost unbearable, made certain she wouldn't be disturbed. Beads of sweat peppered her forehead. Her shirt clung to her abdomen.

Still not sensing a change of direction, Emily prayed. "God," she whispered aloud, "am I making a mistake? Everything points me toward the Kurds. The pathway has opened as easily as all my trips in the past. Am I missing something?

"And what of the Brewingtons?" Tears formed again and she couldn't speak. *One day at a time. I'll take it one day at a time.*

The kitchen door opened causing a vacuum to suck the garage door against its seal. Emily sighed. Her moment of solitude was over.

"Just don't get too attached." Dillon's hushed voice sounded from the other room. "Remember she's here for a short while longer then she'll be helping other kids."

"I wish God didn't need her anywhere else." Jabali's words started a new well of tears. "I bet she'd stay if you married her, Uncle Dillon."

He grunted. "I doubt it."

Chapter Fourteen

Dillon struggled to keep his mind on the morning sermon. Emily sat inside the pew with the children between them. To any untrained eye, they looked like a family. He restrained himself from rubbing his shoulder and crossed his arms over his chest.

The tension between them had only grown since their kiss. How could she ignore what she had to know was there? *God, keep her home. Don't send her away. Send someone else in her place.* Selfish or not, he'd said it. He glanced at Jabali who gave him a weak smile. His little buddy probably said the same prayer.

Lunch held little flair. Dillon cut into his tasteless grilled chicken and forked another piece into his mouth. He looked across the table at his dad. Didn't he ever get tired of eating here? Emily picked at her house salad. Even with carrot swirls and toasted pecans it looked as bland in flavor as the rest of their plates.

He pushed back from the table. "Dad, would you like a pizza?"

His father looked up and blinked. He glanced at the children beside him and then Emily. "Would the rest of you like pizza?"

"Way more than this." Rhysa dropped her fork beside her plate. The children weren't accustomed to eating at the home where his father stayed. Although they often accompanied their dad to visit Mac Brewington, it was never during dinner hours.

At his father's nod, Dillon called in his order. "How about I meet you all by the pond?" The facility may not flavor their food to visitors' liking, but they knew how to landscape. Large shade trees dotted the pond's perimeter with spacious seating. On a day like today with the wind picking up, it made for a relaxing afternoon.

Dillon spoke to several of the elderly residents as he made his way to the entrance. By the time he reached the doors, the deliveryman had stepped from his vehicle and retrieved an insulated bag.

With pizzas in his arms, Dillon strolled around to the pond outside. It wouldn't be fair to the rest of the folks to wake up their taste buds and not have enough to share. The family came into view as he neared the far end. The rare summer breeze cooled the air as it blew over the water.

Emily's hair lifted off her shoulders. She smiled and waved, making sure he knew where they were.

Dillon released a long breath. Despite their circumstances, she didn't hold back and sulk or return hurt for hurt. He knew she wasn't perfect, but in comparison to other women he'd encountered in life, she was perfect for him.

Jabali reached for the boxes and sat them on the concrete picnic table. "Could I say grace?"

"Sure."

Jabali often led grace at home. He seemed to accept the responsibility as his when Robert was gone. "Thank you, Father, for this food and our time of fellowship. Please bless Grandpa's health and help him remember our time together. Amen."

Dillon swallowed and cleared his throat. "That was very nice. Thank you."

His dad looked into Dillon's eyes and smiled. "You've taught him well, son."

Dillon's stomach clenched. Did he remember who he was?

His dad bit into a slice of pepperoni. "Mm-mm. I've been missing this. Remember our Friday nights at the cabin? We'd grab pizzas on our first night there."

He did remember. Dillon's throat tightened. "Yeah, and Robert and I could almost eat a whole one each."

Dad looked from Dillon to Emily. "Something to remember for your marriage. This boy is no light eater."

Emily's face dropped toward her lap. Regaining her composure, she lifted her head to look back at his Dad, but his attention had turned to Rhysa.

Look at me, instead. Dillon wanted to gage her thoughts. To see what emotion her eyes would reveal. Embarrassment, humor, aggravation—he hadn't expected sadness. Gray clouds crowded out the brilliance of her blue eyes. She lifted a corner of her mouth before turning to watch the ducks near the edge of the water. The puny effort of shrugging off his dad's comment held little conviction.

After lunch, Emily took the kids to the truck while Dillon walked his dad back inside. Lainy would be at the house soon, and he didn't want to start her visit with the children off on a bad note because she'd had to wait.

Dad settled into a chair in the foyer. Reluctant to leave while he was still alert, Dillon stalled at the door and looked back. "I love you, Dad." He'd already said the words but they tumbled out again.

"I love you, too, son."

He stepped outside and faced the breeze, took in a deep breath and slowly released it. At the truck, Dillon settled his foot on the floorboard to hoist up into the cab and paused. "Jabali, where's your spider?" He hadn't noticed the ugly toy on his dashboard for quite a while.

"Emily says I won't need it if I trust in my Savior."

Dillon climbed in and looked at Emily sitting beside him. Their eyes held for a long moment. "She's right. That's something we need to apply to every area of life."

She turned away and blinked several times. Between the two of them, they were making a sappy Sunday. If the kids weren't present, he'd urge Emily to divulge the thoughts that caused those tears. Perhaps she no longer wanted the same thing as when she first arrived. Dillon mentally promised to be more sensitive. She was a true soldier for Christ—going wherever she was called. And who was he to stand in God's way?

***

"Emily, it's for you." Jabali held out the phone.

Thankful for the distraction, Emily excused herself from Lainy's criticizing comments. The woman definitely had misplaced jealousy issues. Emily wasn't interested in the husband Lainy acted like she no longer loved. Is that why Robert hadn't asked for a divorce? He knew she still loved him?

"Hello?" She didn't know who would call the house instead of her cell.

"Hey, squirt. I tried calling your cell but you never answered."

"Uncle Tommy?" Though not really her uncle, Tommy Stevenson was her dad's oldest and closet friend and had always been a part of their lives.

"Yeah, it's me. I heard you were home on furlough. We are too, of sorts." Although he headed up a large charitable organization, he often traveled with his family doing short-term mission trips.

Rhysa wandered into the kitchen from the sitting room. She gave Emily a long silent stare before widening her eyes and nodding toward the other room. *Okay, I get it. You don't want to be left alone with your mom. God, help this situation. Soften hearts to one another and to Your Spirit.*

"I've got some things I'd like to discuss with you." Her uncle's voice refocused her attention. "Is now a good time?"

"Actually, no. Could you call back tomorrow?"

There was a pause on the other end of the line. "Maybe. We're heading to Europe in the morning. But this can wait. It was just an idea."

Voices rose in volume from the sitting room.

"Sorry, Uncle Tommy. I want to hear about it—" Rhysa screamed at Lainy then stomped up the stairs.

"O—kay. I think we'd better talk later. Hang in there, kiddo."

Emily took a deep breath before returning the receiver to its base. She rarely heard from her uncle and why of all days did everything have to erupt now? *God give me strength.*

Lainy's head was bent over supported by her hands. Emily considered sitting on the opposite sofa. Although she'd be more comfortable, the scene would be the same as the night she'd wielded the lamp. Not the best memory to bring to the surface, considering the circumstances.

Knowing she was probably setting herself up for more verbal abuse, Emily settled onto the same sofa as Lainy. A verse from Matthew said Christians would be hated for His namesake. Lainy's attacks weren't toward Emily personally. She simply took part in the constant spiritual battle weighed every day.

Jesus, comfort this woman. Help her feel Your presence and understand what it means to take on the helmet of salvation and the sword of the spirit. I don't know where she's at in her spiritual walk with You, but if she hasn't accepted You as her Savior, grow a desire in her heart to want to know You in that personal way and a yearning to learn more from Your Word. Emily raised her head.

"Done?" Lainy's raised brows expressed her impatience. But at least she hadn't interrupted.

"For now." Despite the sarcastic barb, Emily managed a smile. *This isn't about me.*

Lainy blew a sigh between her perfectly painted lips and leaned back against the couch. "Haven't you wanted to run home, yet?"

The thought of the heavenly home awaiting her sent a flood of peace through Emily. But that wasn't what Lainy referred to. "For now, this is my home."

Lainy turned and gave Emily a critical once over. After a long awkward moment, Emily braced herself for more sarcasm. Instead, Lainy's eyes turned shiny with emotion.

"How do you do it?"

If Emily hadn't been sitting near, she might not have heard the whispered query. *Do what? God, I don't want to get off track. Help me give the right answer.* "I ask for help."

Lainy rolled her eyes. "Hmpf. So did I. But you can't get help from someone who's not there."

Prompted by the Spirit, Emily knew she wasn't talking about God, but Robert. "Maybe you should try a different source."

Lainy's eyes narrowed as if Emily had stumbled onto something personal. Something she wasn't supposed to know.

"I meant God. Ask Him."

The woman's features relaxed. "I was never good at the prayer thing. My mind has too much going on to slow down enough for that."

"You could slow down if you wanted to." The glare she received had been expected. Truth was much easier to take when sugarcoated. But Emily sensed a need to hurry. They'd been granted an unusual absence of interruption that the enemy was always eager to end.

"It's a choice. God has far more activity to contend with than we do, yet He chooses to take the time to answer our needs."

"You're really into this God thing aren't you?" Lainy propped an elbow on the back of the sofa and rotated the diamond stud in her ear. "You naive Bible scholar, did you ever consider He's the one who made time, so it's not a stretch for Him to make more to answer all our requests?"

"But He doesn't have to. And you're choosing to miss the point. The sad part is you're not only hurting yourself, but your children."

Lainy's voice trembled as she fought to keep it under control. "What does God have to do with this?" She motioned toward the stairs where Rhysa had stormed to her room.

With Lainy's emotions this high, the Spirit had to be working in her heart. *God, continue fighting for her. Protect her with Your heavenly hosts. Don't allow the enemy's whispering lies to reach her ears.*

"That takes us back to the beginning of our conversation. He gives me the strength and patience to deal with the children in a way that will grow our relationship."

Lainy's throat visibly constricted. The information was received, but how it would be used Emily didn't know. To give Lainy a reprieve from her emotions, Emily changed topics. "Are those the clothes you bought Rhysa?"

Lainy coughed, "Yes, but I might as well return them."

"Stay here for a minute, and let me see if she'll try them on."

Emily slipped her arm beneath the garment bags before Lainy could object. *Keep me from stepping into a viper's pit, God.*

Emily tapped then pushed against the partially open upstairs door. Rhysa always kept it shut when she didn't want to be disturbed.

"Mo—" Rhysa spun from her dresser then plopped onto her bed. "I thought Mom would come up. She hasn't even seen the light Uncle Dillon made." Colors of all sorts radiated against the white ceiling.

"I think she'd like to, but doesn't want to risk upsetting you again."

Rhysa's gaze fell to the garment bags. "Why do you have those?"

"I want to see what they look like."

"Not on me." Rhysa stood and walked toward the other side of the room. "Mom thinks she can turn me into someone I'm not."

Emily unzipped the first bag and pulled out a loose pant and blouse ensemble. The ivory color and silky fabric didn't look like Rhysa but was definitely high quality. She laid it aside and removed the other clothes, all more relaxed.

"Here, try on this one for me, and I'll give you my honest opinion." Emily stepped into the hallway and waited to be called back in.

Rhysa muttered and the sound of a hanger clanked against something in the room. Moments later the door opened. Emily smiled. Though the clothes weren't that of a tree climbing tomboy, they'd been selected with Rhysa's coloring in mind. "I can't object. It looks great on you."

Although it seemed she didn't want it to show, Rhysa possessed a stronger feminine nature than she wanted to admit. She shut the door commenting on trying on the next garment without any encouragement from Emily.

The ivory slacks and blouse were last. Rhysa called from inside. "I'm ready."

A small gasp blew past Emily's lips. The color did more for Rhysa than she would've guessed.

Rhysa stood looking in the mirror. "It doesn't suit me."

"It fits perfectly." Emily moved her gaze to the tightly worn ponytail. "Can I take your hair down for a minute?"

The mirror reflected the girl's frown. "I guess."

Emily worked the elastic loose and brushed her fingers through thick, shiny locks. They fell in a wave framing Rhysa's perfectly symmetrical face.

"Wow! You're pretty, Rhysa." Jabali stood in the doorway smiling. "I like your hair down." He turned toward his room and left them alone.

"I'll never have a place to wear this."

"Hmm …" Emily thought of her sister Lucy and Dorin, the Romanian. If her intuition was right—"It'd be perfect for a wedding."

Rhysa's eyes widened as a smile stretched across her face. She jumped and clapped her hands. "You mean—you and Uncle Dillon?"

"N-No." Emily cringed. How could one thought lead to such a misunderstanding? She placed her hand on Rhysa's arm and softened her voice. "You know I can't stay."

The air thinned as Rhysa's face crumbled. She dropped her head, but couldn't hide a sob that hiccupped from her throat. Before Emily could react, Rhysa turned and fell against her in a torment of tears. It was the first time Emily was the recipient of the girl's affections, but at a costly reward.

A stabbing pain pierced her heart. In all her years of missionary work, no child had entwined their way into her heart quite like Rhysa and her brother.

Rhysa's shoulders shook as she stuttered, "I wish you were my mom. I don't want you to leave."

As if embarrassed, she pulled back from Emily's arms. She shuffled toward the window and wiped her face. "I know," Rhysa drew a halting breath, "I know you're needed elsewhere, but I wish we didn't have to share you."

Sweeter words couldn't have been spoken. Emily dried her own face as she heard a knock from the front door. "We better see who that is."

Emily walked ahead of both children toward the stairs.

"Mark!" Lainy's surprised voice fell to a whisper. "What are you doing here?"

Chapter Fifteen

Emily backed the kids away from the stairs. before Lainy or Mark could notice them.

Why would Lainy question Mark's presence in a whisper? What did they have to hide?

Emily swallowed hard. Things were starting to fall into place, in a dreadful way. *Please don't allow Lainy to be involved. That would be more than the children could take.*

Rhysa inched nearer the stairs, her head bent forward to listen. Emily had to distract her and Jabali before their suspicions built past the facts.

Emily sniffed the air. For several weeks, an offending odor would heckle her senses, but she could never find its source. "There's a funny smell up here. Let's find it before we go downstairs."

"It's not from my room. Try Jabali's." Rhysa, distracted from the front door scene, followed Emily toward her brother's room.

There wasn't much out of place save for a few shirts and socks on the floor. Did she dare? Emily picked up a sock and brought it to her nose.

"Phew, but not the phew I'm looking for."

Jabali giggled. "You're crazy."

Beside the bed, the smell increased. Leaning closer, she ruled out the pillow. She dropped to her knees and the smell overwhelmed her. Beneath the bed against the wall, was a paper plate of left-over food.

Emily pinched her nose and slid the plate out and into the waste basket. She tied the bag shut while holding her breath.

Hoarding. A common problem with orphans who've had to fight for food.

"Let's go swimming, Rhysa!" Jabali, either embarrassed by Emily's find or wanting to avoid a lecture he'd probably heard before, ran down the stairs.

Rhysa fanned the air in front of her. "I agree with him. It doesn't stink outside."

Emily followed her and tossed the foul bag into the trashcan outside. Back in the house she stopped beside Lainy at the kitchen window.

Jabali's skinny arms swung the water hose in the air above him.

"He's watering himself. Maybe he'll grow." Emily watched Rhysa run from the hose's reach and jump in the pool.

"He needs to grow." Lainy's voice held a note of concern. "Next to Rhysa he looks a lot younger than ten years old."

Emily nodded in agreement as she collected the kitchen trash to set outside with the other. Jabali's hoarding issue would have to be addressed. But she'd wait and talk it over with Dillon. The thought to share with Lainy crossed her mind. But Lainy would likely take offense and see it as an attack against her lack of mothering.

It seemed every time Emily made strides with either child the devil would insure at least one set back.

Missions were just as trying, but in a different sense. Training adults, her job didn't require constant interaction with children. Although she worked with many of them in between helping teach their teachers, time didn't allow for strong attachments.

This job wouldn't allow her such freedoms. The strings of her heart were already weaving themselves around Jabali and Rhysa.

Emily found Lainy in a shaded lounge by the pool. She joined her and enjoyed the comfortable silence as they watched the kids with their new water toys. For the fifth time, Rhysa dove to collect the rings Jabali had thrown.

For a girl who'd never swum before coming to the Brewington's, Rhysa had easily taken to the water. With little splashing she slipped below and maneuvered toward the bottom, moving her body like a beaver.

Rhysa came up for air and glanced in Emily's direction, yet again. The same thing happened each time she broke the surface. Either she wanted to ensure a constant audience, or the girl had a plan she didn't want known by the adults. The children's voices dropped in volume. Emily strained to overhear.

"Keep Mom busy, and don't let her in the house." Rhysa wriggled from her brother's grasp and shoved his tube away.

Jabali paddled his hands to return to her side. "Rhysa, I don't want you getting caught."

"I won't," she hissed, "as long as you do what I told you." She swam to the side of the pool and hoisted herself out.

Lainy smiled. "Are you done swimming?"

"No. I'll be back." Rhysa glanced from her mom to Emily as she dried off.

Yes, Rhysa was definitely up to something.

Rhysa had confided enough, Emily knew what the girl was capable of once her mind was set. Earlier in the summer, Rhysa shared a story about a sick boy she'd known in the orphanage. He'd been told there wasn't any medicine for him, but Rhysa knew differently. She said because of his disabilities the workers hadn't wanted to waste the medicine on him.

She'd filled the hole in the office door-jam with tissue to keep the lock from engaging. Long after everyone had gone to sleep, Rhysa snuck back and rummaged through the director's purse for the key to the medicine cabinet, kept locked above the desk.

She stole the medicine and the boy survived.

Pride and purpose had filled Rhysa's voice as she told the story. What purpose fueled her now?

Emily excused herself from the pool and entered the kitchen. "What are you doing?"

Rhysa whipped around to where Emily stood inside the door. "I—I needed a drink. Now I'm going to use the bathroom, then I'll be back."

Emily narrowed her eyes as she gave a slow nod. Lainy's purse sat on the counter behind Rhysa. Had she been rummaging through it? Emily's stomach tightened. She'd never caught Rhysa stealing before, surely she wouldn't start now.

Voices from the office filtered their way into the kitchen. Could Mark's presence be cause for Rhysa's suspicious behavior? He obviously made her uncomfortable. But that didn't explain the conversation Emily overheard in the pool.

Whatever she was doing, Emily hadn't caught her, and without making a scene, there wasn't much else she could do.

Guide her decisions, God. Emily smiled as if she suspected nothing. They'd talk later. "Why don't you bring the pitcher of lemonade with you when you come?"

"Sure." Rhysa took a sip from a glass on the counter.

Emily returned to the pool and sat on the edge of the concrete. Jabali avoided looking her direction. Clearly, the children had something on their minds they didn't want to share.

Their scheming didn't necessarily mean they were up to something bad. Emily had formed plenty of plans with her siblings that excluded the adults. The thought brought a smile to her face and eased her worries.

Although Lucy wasn't a mother yet, their brothers had their hands full with children.

Keaton had inherited two girls and four boys when he married. And from numerous stories he and his wife, Lindsey, shared, a week didn't go by without incident.

The door slammed shut as Rhysa returned to the pool.

Emily looked up from where she sat with her feet dangling in the pool. "Where's the lemonade?"

Rhysa's blue gaze darkened to gray. For a long moment she stared without blinking.

Did she think Emily knew what she'd been up to?

"I forgot." She blinked and her features softened. "I'll go get it."

What was she hiding?

Moments later Rhysa returned with the pitcher and glasses.

"When's your dad coming home again?" Lainy stretched her arms toward her toes.

Rhysa jerked her head up as she poured their glasses, spilling the lemonade. It ran through the mesh iron of the table splattering off the concrete onto her legs.

"I can't remember." She turned to Emily. "Do you know?"

Emily breathed a sigh of relief. Although she wished Lainy could be trusted, she was glad Rhysa knew not to take the chance.

"The last few weeks have been pretty busy. I'll have to check my calendar or ask Dillon." Emily held a level breath. Lainy didn't need to suspect anything. Until they had proof of who wanted Robert dead and why, no one could be trusted.

Lainy accepted the drink from Rhysa and took a sip while watching Emily. "You seem to have brought that brother-in-law of mine out of his shell."

Emily shrugged.

"I imagine he's going to miss you when you leave next month."

"Don't talk about her leaving!"

They both turned to look at Jabali. It was uncommon to hear him raise his voice. He pulled his mask over his face and dove beneath the water.

Guilt descended on Emily like a rain-soaked cloud. She'd never dealt with this much indecision.

"Having trouble figuring things out?" Lainy almost sounded like she cared, but Emily knew that would be too far of a jump in one day's time.

"Welcome to the club." The woman's sarcastic nature proved Emily right.

God, I only have a month left. What am I missing? Even as she prayed, she knew part of the problem. Where she used to converse with God easily, now an increasing fog robbed her of clarity. Almost as if the desire to stay had built a fear of how He might respond, thus deafening her ears to His voice. *I know I should want Your will over mine, but what if Your will is for me to leave? Would you do that to the kids?* She inwardly cringed. What was she thinking? God didn't fall for guilt trips. And she should know better than to resort to such tactics.

Warriors of the faith were often seen as people above temptation, as their role protected them from common weakness. But the enemy never acted with mercy. Temptations, no matter what form, challenged everyone. And right now, Emily's heart was sorely tempted.

Memories of her step-mom's stories floated to mind. As a nanny at one time herself, Ann's attachment to the children had caused problems to surface that might have been avoided had she listened to God. Was Emily making the same mistake?

If she stayed, the children's attachment to her might override any restoration possible with their adopted mother. That is, if Lainy planned to continue her relationship with them.

She glanced at Lainy who'd sat forward in the chair, still poised as if for a photo shoot. Did she even know how to be a mom? Were the children safe under her care?

Searching for reasons to stay by targeting the nearest person wasn't showing godly character. Emily sighed and ran her fingers through her hair. She was failing fast. How easy it was to follow closely to God when surrounded by other likeminded people. Even though overseas missions weren't pretty, sharing the same urgent passion for the salvation of souls with co-workers created strength unlike any she'd experienced in the states.

The men's voices floated from the front yard. Mark must be getting ready to go. Had Dillon discovered any leads? He'd staged the meeting with the intention of getting a better read on the family friend.

Lainy stood and smoothed the creases of her pants. "I've been here long enough. I'll call later and find out when Robert will be home. Do you have his number? I think it's changed."

Emily stared for a moment not sure how to answer. "I don't have it." It was the truth. She'd never needed to call with Dillon available.

"I'll ask Dillon."

The temptation to ask the woman why burned Emily's tongue. Did Lainy want to get back with Robert, or was she only trying to pin his location? The thought might be unfair, but what she'd witnessed between Lainy and Mark at the door still didn't seem innocent. And if Lainy was the culprit, then she wasn't fit to be a mother ... and Emily didn't need to leave.

Right, God?

"Snack time." Emily called to the kids.

They hopped out of the water and ran to the house.

Emily followed Lainy into the kitchen. The air conditioning formed goose bumps along Rhysa and Jabali's arms. But after their snack of cookies and milk they'd probably be back in the pool. Emily smiled as they wrapped towels like blankets around their bodies.

Dillon met them as Lainy picked up her purse and frowned. "You're not leaving."

"Actually, I am."

"No, you're not. Robert will be here any minute and we're all going to sit down and have a nice talk."

"Robert's coming?"

Emily couldn't miss the lilt in Lainy's voice. If it weren't for her possible treachery, Emily would've felt pity toward her.

***

Emily busied herself in the kitchen with dinner. Occupied by the children, Lainy stayed upstairs while the kids showed off their new lighting. A yelling match had yet to be heard. Prayers were being answered.

"What smells so good?" Dillon passed through the kitchen as if to go to the shop and paused by the center island.

"Lasagna. It's simple and comforting."

"Good choice. Maybe it will calm the storm before it develops."

Her thoughts exactly. Though she told herself not to, she raised her eyes to his and the room immediately shrunk. All their time together reeled before her in one heart wrenching moment. Would he wait for her? If God called her home within a couple years, would he still be here willing to offer his heart as he was now?

"You're water's going to—"

Emily turned to see the pan of noodles boil over. The foamy water sizzled as it met with the heated coil of the burner sending steam clouds up into the air.

Dillon whipped past her and grabbed the potholders from her hands before she could react. He set the pot on the back burner then she turned it down.

Her face warmed with shame. "I do that a lot when I'm home."

"You don't make the same mistake overseas?"

"I'm normally not allowed to cook." She snickered at her lack of expertise.

"So you travel with the same people each time."

"No. Everyone just seems to figure it out rather quickly."

Dillon's smile touched his eyes. As if they'd reached a normal flow between them again, he glanced at the gathered contents on the counter and asked, "What can I do to help?"

"Aside from saving Maurita's kitchen from certain disaster, you can cook the meat."

The warmth of the kitchen grew not so much from the heat of the oven as from the contentment between Emily and Dillon. After a week of awkward interactions she was eager to regain their friendship.

With a quick peep into the sitting room to assure their privacy, Emily approached the subject of Mark. "Did you learn anything from your meeting?"

Dillon tensed. "We had an open chat with Robert on the speaker phone that got a bit heated. Mark doesn't like the idea that business growth has been delayed and wants to head up the conventions in place of Robert."

"Sounds controlling for a guy who isn't part owner." Emily added a pinch of sugar and extra basil to the Italian tomato sauce.

"That's what I'm thinking." He leaned against the counter and continued in a hushed tone. "If he's our guy, then how can killing Robert gain him anything? It doesn't make sense."

"Does he know you're not part owner?"

Dillon nodded.

Emily swallowed and said a prayer for guidance. She never wanted to falsely accuse anyone, but they had to look at every possible angle. "Do you think he's interested in Lainy?"

Dillon blinked then narrowed his eyes as if considering the idea for the first time. "Lainy?" He voiced her name with disgust.

"If Robert died, the business would become hers, right?" She continued after his nod. "Then if he married her ..."

"Ah ha! I see where you're going."

"Uncle Dillon, Emily," Rhysa hovered in the kitchen entryway before taking hesitant steps toward them. "I have something you need to look at ... but don't be mad."

Chapter Sixteen

Dillon slid the memory card from Rhysa's camera into the computer not knowing what to expect. His niece inched toward the door. "Not so fast. What am I looking at?"

Rhysa turned her head and looked toward the stairs. "She doesn't know."

"Who doesn't?" Emily answered from behind Dillon.

Rhysa put a finger to her lips to signal for them to keep quiet. "Mom. It's pictures from her phone." Without asking permission, she left the room and climbed the stairs.

"Did you know she did this?" Dillon watched the bar turn green as the contents of the card loaded into the computer then clicked to open the folder.

"No." Emily glanced from the computer screen to Dillon. "I thought she was up to something when she left the pool. But I checked on her and didn't find anything wrong." Her eyes trailed back to the screen as she peered closer.

Dillon frowned. "Whoa. Who is she texting? Mark!" A picture of his boat appeared beside his texts.

"Shh." Emily touched his shoulder and pointed to the empty stairs.

Dillon quieted and clicked on a photo of an open text.

Lainy—*"I can't understand why he doesn't stay home. Am I not enough?"*

Mark—*"You are to me. Let him go, and let's move in together."*

Lainy—*"I don't know. Wait til I decide to divorce him or not."*

Mark—*"Divorces are nasty. We don't need that yet."*

Dillon leaned back against the chair. Learning the truth could be a painful process. He clicked a different picture and saw another screen listing texts with Mark. She definitely depended on Mark as a friend, but did it go further than that? Without the access to all the texts there was no way of knowing for sure if their Mark's relationship was more than platonic. Though Dillon had lost most of his respect for his sister-in-law, he still hoped she hadn't gone that far.

"From the sound of things, this might be the reason for the attempts against Robert, just like you guessed. Outside of our accountant, Mark knows better than anyone the worth of the company. He wouldn't want Lainy to divorce Robert and chance not inheriting his money maker."

Emily scrunched her freckled nose. "Could he be capable of that—of killing his friend? He seemed like a decent guy."

"Maybe not directly, but I wouldn't put it past him to hire someone to do the job." His chest seized with an icy dread as he recounted the events leading up to now. Why had it taken them this long to figure it out?

Robert could have easily died while his murderer took over his life.

Dillon read the other pictures then clicked print. He ground his teeth together as anger boiled beneath his skin. How long had Lainy leaned on Mark as a friend? Why hadn't she communicated with her husband? Although Robert was often gone, he called home each day to talk to the family—until Lainy stopped answering the phone.

Time for naivety had lapsed. Robert had to face facts whether he liked it or not.

"Can we pray about this?"

Emily's soft-spoken question pierced through his growing indignation. Eager to take control, he hadn't considered going to the cross. He bit back the desire to advance on his own. Had she not stopped him, he would've plowed ahead in anger. But God didn't approach obstacles with emotion. He approached them with truth.

"Where should we start?"

"Let's suit up with the armor of God."

Dillon scratched his head, straining to remember the passage from Ephesians. "Your idea. You lead." He followed her action and bowed his head.

"God, we realize we're in the midst of a battle. We need your helmet of salvation to keep our thoughts centered on the facts and not be led astray by the enemy. Protect our feelings, including Robert's, with the breastplate of your righteousness and govern us with Your truth …"

With his head bowed, Dillon listened as Emily asked for God's hand and guidance. This was the first time they'd prayed together. The first time he'd prayed aloud with anyone. Instead of feeling awkward as he expected, a natural ease enveloped the room. Could he have opportunities like this?

After Emily's prayer he knew he couldn't use the printed proof. At least not yet. If Dillon wanted his brother in a strong frame of mind, Lainy had to offer the information.

The timer for the lasagna buzzed, calling Emily away. Dillon shut down the computer and printer as Jabali tromped down the stairs followed by Lainy and Rhysa. Lainy's ability to stay focused on the children for this long surprised him. If it weren't for the evidence from her phone, he'd almost think she was trying to change.

Rhysa caught his attention with a questioning look. He waited for Lainy to pass the office then motioned for Rhysa to join him. She lagged behind until her brother and mother were in the kitchen.

"How did you get these?" He ejected the memory card from the computer.

Rhysa's face tightened as she stared hard at Dillon. "Am I in trouble? I didn't read the stuff. I just took the pictures."

Dillon moved closer and gently placed the card in her hand. "No. You're not in trouble. But I don't want you getting caught and in trouble by someone else."

Rhysa nodded but kept her gaze diverted. "I slipped in when you were talking to Mark and found Mom's phone in her purse."

She glanced behind her before continuing. "I brought it to my room and took the pictures."

Stealthy like a cat, he'd never known she'd gone past the office. Had she been scared or worried she'd be seen? Dillon studied her expression, but the kid was an expert at hiding her emotions.

"Don't mention this to anyone." Dillon unlocked the drawer to the files and hid the papers in the back. "After dinner, you and Jabali go to my cottage with Emily while the rest of us talk."

Rhysa stared at the wall past Dillon then finally looked back. As if challenging him for the truth, her eyes drilled into his. "Will Dad divorce her?" The old Rhysa threatened to return as a means of self-preservation. The trust that had recently softened her features faded to an almost imperceptible level.

Before Emily's involvement with the family, and her ability to draw him away from his work, Rhysa's question might not have triggered Dillon's recognition of her fear. But things had changed. Because he cared, he easily saw through her. The girl wasn't as tough as she pretended. Nor did Rhysa want her new family broken more than it already was.

Dillon clenched his jaw. "Don't jump to conclusions. God's still in control." His comment came out unexpectedly, but after Emily's prayer, his anger had changed to concern.

Before they could join the others, the garage door opened, and Jabali yelled, "Dad!"

Rhysa spun out of the office and toward the kitchen, her excited voice mimicking her brother.

Robert always arrived to the fan-fare of his children. The stark difference each parent received in greetings from the children should be a wake-up call for Lainy. Maybe it had been and her visits were a result of wanting to change.

Dillon relieved the lasagna dish from Emily's hands and placed it on the table. Then he set out dinnerware as an excuse to watch the interchange between his brother and Lainy. In his usual respectful manner,

Robert leaned forward and placed a kiss on Lainy's cheek.

"I'm glad you stayed." As if soaking in her presence, his brother's focus never wavered from Lainy. *Boy, was he in for a world of hurt.* "I didn't think you would."

Her jaw tightened as her lips stretched in a taunt line. Dillon expected a verbal explosion but she remained quiet and took a seat.

How long had it been since the whole family sat together at the table? Dillon thought back and knew it had to be before the shooting in the woods. To his knowledge, Lainy still didn't know of his injury.

"… and Uncle Dillon says I'm a good helper. He's glad to have me in the shop …" Jabali, unaware of the strain between his parents, talked incessantly. No doubt excited over seeing his parents together again.

"This is great, Emily." Dillon helped himself to a second scoop and ribbed her in front of the others. "As long as she has supervision, she's an awesome cook."

Along with his brother and the children, he enjoyed her humorous explanation of the minor incident on the stove. Lainy fought a smile as she seemingly tried to retain a look of dull interest. Clearly, she still wasn't a fan of the nanny her husband hired. Could it be she was jealous? Dillon glanced between her and his brother. Though strained, their love for one another was still evident.

Jabali, now full, pushed back his chair. "Oh, I almost forgot. Here's your phone, Mom. Thanks for letting me play the game." He pulled it from his pocket and left the phone beside her before leaving to play in the sitting room.

Had Jabali asked to play the game on the phone because he'd really wanted to, or had it been for a diversion—to draw his mother's attention away from her texting and back to him and Rhysa? It mattered little now, as the truth would soon come out.

Without his chatter, no one else seemed to know what to say. The silence grew awkward.

"How long were you gone this time?" Lainy drew her eyes from her phone to stare at Robert, waiting for an answer. Although she maintained a friendly expression, her motive was clear. The fight had begun.

Robert set down his fork. "I could ask you the same thing."

"I left because you were never home." Her voice rose with indignation. She pushed back her chair as if ready to leave. "Nothing's changed, and I see no reason why you wanted me here."

"Stay put." Robert's deepened voice made everyone pause. "Kids, go upstairs please."

Rhysa looked at Dillon. He'd told her to go to his house.

Emily rose, "I'll take them to the cottage."

"No. You're staying, too." Robert pointed a finger from Emily back to her seat. "Your car was tampered with. You're just as involved as I am, and it's time we got answers."

Dillon knew she was uncomfortable with the situation, as was he. But Robert's new demeanor didn't leave room for questioning. Emily returned to her seat as Rhysa hurried out of the room. Jabali was heard heading up the stairs.

Lainy fidgeted with her phone and glanced between Robert and Emily. "What do you mean her car was tampered with?"

"There's a lot you either need to know, or you already know. I'm not sure." Robert addressed Lainy.

"Either way, you can start by explaining who you've been keeping company with."

Her eyes narrowed. "What's it matter to you?"

"You're still my wife, Lainy. It matters." Robert ground out his words and reached across the table with his opened palm. "May I see that?"

"No." Lainy instinctively drew the phone toward her. "I don't see why you're making a fuss."

"You stopped talking to me several months ago. Who have you been talking to if it hasn't been me?"

Lainy's tongue darted across her lips. "A friend." Her well-manicured fingers flipped a lock of hair as her confidence grew. "And he listens better than you ever did."

"Why? Because he tells you what you want to hear rather than the truth?"

"He makes time for me." Her voice wavered.

"Does he also pay your rent and support your shopping habits?"

Her eyes seemed to battle between giving into anger and facing the truth.

Mark wasn't about to let someone else spend his money. His Santa list could put most children to shame. Honesty would also argue the fact that Mark could never give Lainy the attention she desired—the attention she craved from Robert.

Dillon looked up from the table and caught Emily's gaze. She seemed to want an escape as much as he did. This was personal and didn't involve either of them.

"Why do you think I work so hard to grow the business?" Robert's voice softened. He gave her time for thought. "To give you things you never had."

The hurt in Robert's eyes ran deeper than any Dillon had suffered. His brother loved Lainy. He loved her enough to sacrifice his wants to supply hers. He loved her enough to spend hours away from the family he'd wanted for so long. And he loved her enough to let her go when she claimed she needed space.

Dillon ran a thumbnail along a crack in the wood table. He'd only recently begun to consider the stirrings in his heart toward Emily as love. But was it as strong as the love Robert felt for Lainy? Could Dillon love Emily enough to let her go?

"Is it Mark?"

Dillon raised his head. His brother had jumped ahead without any help from him.

A light shimmer formed in Lainy's eyes before she covered it with a hardened expression.

"Has he asked you to marry him?"

Lainy shifted her attention to Emily, ignoring Robert. "What happened to your car? He said you're in this too. In what?"

Emily swallowed and glanced from Robert to Dillon. "Someone is trying to hurt your family." She turned to face Lainy. "Is that what you want?"

Lainy frowned. "What?"

"Someone's been trying to kill Robert," Dillon interjected.

Lainy's eyes widened before her forehead furrowed. "Why? How?"

Dillon rose from the table. He had to move around. The uncomfortable situation was made worse by Lainy's proposed innocence. Either she didn't know anything about the attempts or she knew how to act.

He spoke as he paced the room. "That someone also drilled a hole in Emily's oil tank that could've caused a major accident on the freeway—involving your kids." He let the phrase sink in.

Lainy's eyes darted from each of them. She began to shake her head. "I don't know anything about this. Are you actually accusing me?" Her clipped words upheld her innocence. "Why would I want you dead, Robert?"

***

Emily sought an escape from the escalating drama. Although Robert thought she should stay, she didn't see how her presence could make a difference. She slipped out through the kitchen door. The temperature hadn't cooled, but the air breathed easier than inside. Her parents had never dealt with such heavy friction. At least not to Emily's knowledge. What made the difference?

Two people devoted to God.

In a recent conversation, Robert assured Emily Lainy had accepted Jesus as her savior. If so, then an unseen battle had distracted her attention from the cross.

Shop Cat bounded from the side of the house. His meow hiccupped with each bounce of his paws. Emily met him halfway and squatted to her knees as he slipped into her arms. She relished the feline's soft fur against her face and the sound of his purr next to her ear. Life as a cat had never appealed to her as much as it did now.

A prayer waited on the end of her tongue, but Emily couldn't move past the heaviness in her heart. How could two people fall so far from where they began? She formed a short prayer. *There's still time, Lord. Guide her back to You. Fight for her. And rekindle a love in her heart for her husband.*

She started to rise to her feet as a hand clamped onto her shoulder, forcing her to stay put.

"Don't make a sound." The voice didn't belong to Dillon or Robert. Emily stiffened and Shop Cat scratched his way out of her arms. "It's important you do everything you can to discourage Lainy from moving back home. The children's lives depend on your success."

Anger heated her senses. The trials of the Brewington family were enough to deal with. She wasn't in the mood to add assault to the list. Whoever was behind her didn't have the right to threaten her or the children.

Emily grabbed the man's wrist pinning her down and tried to twist free. A sharp pain formed as something round jabbed her in the back.

"I wouldn't try anything if I were you."

"Then you shouldn't have threatened the children!" Drawing on defense classes she'd taken in preparation of living overseas, she reached her other hand over his head. In one powerful thrust, she rolled forward bringing him with her.

She twisted to gain sight of her assailant. Before Emily could regain her footing, a sharp blow against her head knocked her back to the ground.

Chapter Seventeen

"Oof!" Emily fell on her shoulder, her head bounced off the grass. The world turned blurry as hot lightening flared inside her skull. *What just happened?* She froze in place and willed the pain to subside.

The longer she stayed on the lawn, the more time she gave the culprit. Emily blinked and opened her eyes knowing he'd be gone. She struggled to her knees.

Someone's hands touched her back. She flung her arms and kicked wildly as she tried to stand.

"Emily, it's me."

The spinning world slowed as her eyes focused on Dillon. "Where is he?"

"Where is who?"

"The creep who hit me?" She staggered as she fought the fuzzy feeling in her head. "Follow his tracks."

"I would if I was a bloodhound, but I'm more concerned about you."

Her eyes searched wildly for some sign that would tell which way he'd gone. "He's been here before. I can feel it."

"Again, who?" Dillon's concern grew in his voice. "What happened?"

"What type of watch does Mark wear?" Emily rested her hands on Dillon's arms for balance. "Does it have a rectangle face that's curved to his wrist?"

She knew she'd hit her target. Concern turned to anger as Dillon's focus switched from her to the yard, searching for her attacker. "Let's get inside and you can explain what happened." He kept one hand on her arm to steady her. Emily knew she enjoyed his protective response more than she should, but now wasn't the time to argue with herself.

They stepped into the kitchen and were thrust back into Robert and Lainy's heated debate. The pounding in Emily's head increased with a vengeful intensity.

Neither could see the truth of the battle. Blinded by the fallen state of the world, they still thought it was about them.

Emily hadn't walked in their shoes. Having never married, she didn't have the qualifications to tell them how to run their marriage. But God did.

The triangle her youth pastor had once drawn made perfect sense. With God at the top and each spouse on either side of the bottom corners, he'd drawn two arrows starting from the bottom angling upward. If each person lived their life striving to grow closer to God, they'd naturally grow closer to one another.

Too bad I don't have a dry erase board.

"Stop!" Emily pressed against the tender spot on her head. "All of this," she waved her hands to include the phone and the garage where Robert's car was parked, "it's all a distraction to distance you from God."

If only they could catch a glimpse of the unseen war raging around them. The enemy with his fiery darts aimed at their hearts and God's army fitted with shields and swords fighting for His children.

"Each of you could build a compelling case based on offenses and rejection, but the reality is this isn't about flesh and blood. The battle is spiritual. The devil has you in his court completely focused on yourselves, your wants, your needs, your hurts."

With sudden alarm, Emily became aware of the astonished faces of her audience. She chanced losing her job, but their arguing had to come to an end. Her head continued to throb. More important matters were at stake.

"I realize it takes two to turn your situation around. But for the children's sake, you both need to do exactly that. Someone just attacked ... what's that?" Emily peered at the phone on the wall. Something small and round protruded from the bottom of the receiver.

Dillon moved toward the wall as Robert rose from his chair. After peeling it off, he held up something no bigger than a dime. Robert took the item from Dillon's hand and plunked it into a glass of tea.

Silence filled the room. Emily glanced at Dillon. What was it? Robert answered her unspoken question. "A listening device. And I can guess who planted it here."

Like flipping through the pages of a book, recent events passed through Emily's mind. That's how Mark knew when they were gone. Everything worth discussing had been done in the kitchen. He could've easily overheard every plan they made. And that's why he'd threatened Emily—he'd overhead Lainy and Robert's discussion.

"I'm checking the children." Emily left the room.

***

Dillon grabbed the phone off the hook and dialed the police station. Ten minutes passed before he hung up in frustration. "All their units are out on call. She said she'd report the incident."

Lainy filled her glass at the sink. Her cosmopolitan appearance marred by stress. Mussed hair stood up on the back of her head. Dark circles gathered beneath her eyes. She slumped against the counter. "I don't understand why you think Mark is doing this. What could he possibly have to gain?"

Her appearance must have pulled at Robert's heartstrings. He joined her on the other side of the kitchen and pulled her into an embrace. Though he spoke quietly, Dillon heard him explain how his death could open the door for Mark—through Lainy. She crumpled into his arms and wept.

Dillon entered the office and closed the door. *God, we need direction.* After turning on the computer and looking through the search engine, he realized two things. One, if they wanted Mark's phone records to prove he had connections with a hired gun, they'd have to be subpoenaed. Two, they didn't have that much time.

Mark's fear of losing control would prove to be his failure. His slip with Emily hinted as much. Dillon accessed the security cameras. Bingo. The camera caught Mark as he rounded the garage. "Ha!" Dillon peered closer at the screen. But the scene he expected to play out never happened. The rotating camera had turned and caught the stillness of the shop.

He slammed his fist onto the desk. Mark must have studied the cameras enough to know their movements and timing. Would they ever catch him in a mistake? Dillon rubbed his shoulder as he stormed from the office.

Emily sat nestled on the couch with her legs tucked under her. "What's wrong?"

He released a deep sigh. "The cameras didn't catch him."

"I didn't figure they would." She leaned her head back against the cushion.

He stared, trying to detect if she suffered a concussion. If only he'd gone out sooner. A small voice had warned him not to let her go alone.

His chest tightened. Soon she'd be alone in a foreign world where any number of Marks might be waiting to attack. Although he didn't know exactly where her next mission was stationed, many countries still considered Christianity a crime. An offense worthy of death.

He touched her head, letting his hand smooth over her soft hair. "Do you feel okay?"

Emily glanced up where he stood behind the sofa. Pleasure over his concern seemed to radiate from her eyes. "I'm fine." Then she shrugged breaking the intimacy. "Wrestling calves and hogs on a farm all my life must have prepared me for such events."

Let's hope that's the last of "such events." Emily made it clear she didn't want to explore their attraction. But Dillon didn't agree. If his concern mattered to her, why did she run from her feelings?

The answer became clear. In the end, he wouldn't want to settle for a long distance relationship. She knew he'd pressure her to stay … and perhaps she'd surrender to the temptation. But building a relationship on regrets wouldn't help either of them.

Lainy and Robert each took a seat across from Emily. Although they didn't hold hands, it seemed they still drew strength from being near each other. Maybe there was hope for their marriage.

Dillon straddled the arm of the couch.

"I had no idea about any of this." Lainy's eyes were swollen from crying. "I told Robert I'd end all contact with Mark. Immediately."

Dillon waved his hand. "You can't do that or he'll—"

"Dillon's right." Emily interrupted. "He's too unbalanced right now, and he threatened the kids' safety. Keep talking to him. Act as though everything is fine."

"No." Robert leaned forward. "I won't let her put herself at risk."

"Listen to Rhysa's plan—"

"You told Rhysa about this?" Robert narrowed his eyes. "How much?"

"Rhysa has lived a lifetime in her short twelve years. Don't underestimate her. All I did was fill in a few questions. She had the rest figured out." Emily sat forward on the cushion. "Robert, you pretend to go on another trip. Lainy, you leak it to Mark. String your relationship along but at a distance. Meanwhile, Dillon invites him back here for business where we take pictures of the files on his phone."

Robert asked, "How do we do that?"

Emily glanced at Dillon. They both knew not to mention Rhysa taking Lainy's phone. "The kids know how."

"I don't like it." Lainy ran her fingers through her hair. "Any number of things could go wrong. We need to wait for the police."

Dillon explained how long it would take for any action to take place. "All the time, the hit man would still be trying to earn the promised money."

"Whatever we decide, Lainy," Robert turned to his wife, "we'll have to let you know later. If you stay any longer, Mark will become more suspicious. Go home and act like you still believe in him when he calls."

The rest of the evening wore long into the night as they formed a plan and informed Lainy through a phone call. In two nights with Robert safely tucked away in a nearby motel, Dillon would call Mark.

***

"Whew, what's wrong with the air conditioning?" Mark slipped his jacket off as soon as he reached the office.

Dillon closed the door partway then rubbed his damp temples. "Something with the unit. We'll have someone look at it this afternoon." That someone would be Dillon when he turned the unit on again. So far, their plan was running like clockwork.

He took his seat and turned to the open screen. "I called you out here for a reason, Mark. Robert's falling apart at the seams."

Dillon swiveled the chair to stare at the picture of his sister-in-law Robert kept on the desk. "He found out about your friendship with Lainy." Dillon held out a hand. "I didn't bring you here to talk about your involvement with her, but about my brother. The poor guy's not in any shape to run the business and it's starting to show."

Just as they'd planned, Mark swung at the pitch. "I knew it was coming to this." As if Dillon had never mentioned Lainy, Mark attacked the subject of business. "I have a few shows I can still get us in before the end of summer. I'll sign us up and attend them myself."

Dillon drummed his fingers on top of the desk. "Okay." He slowed his speech as if giving the idea time for thought. Mark had been too quick with a solution, leaving the kids stretched for time to complete their part. "Why don't we start with one show and go from there?"

His question started a debate Dillon knew he could drag out long enough for Jabali to crawl in and retrieve Mark's phone or truck keys from his jacket pocket. If all Jabali found were keys, then Rhysa would look for the phone in the truck and snap similar photos like she had with her mom's phone. Their whole plan depended on Mark having the phone with him.

Mark continued to argue. "I still think you should trust me with three shows. I know by the time the first one is finished, you'll wish you'd given me a longer leash."

Keep talking, rookie. Let something slip. "And why's that?"

An evil glint flickered in Mark's eyes before he exhaled and stretched his arms to rest his hands on the back of his head. "Because of the success I'll bring to Brewington Lighting and Displays."

Dillon inwardly sighed. Mark was smooth enough he hadn't made a slip, and Dillon wasn't convinced their culprit was fooled.

***

Emily paced the soft carpeting in her bedroom waiting for the children to return. It seemed their mission was taking forever. Mark would notice the unusually quiet house, but would he suspect anything? If he found out, they'd all be in danger.

She stood in front of the open window and looked out over the field. Nothing moved. The world seemed to hold its breath with them anticipating what would happen next. She moved away from the window and opened her closet. Staring at the few items hanging above her single suitcase, she realized in only a couple of weeks she'd be gone, the closet empty.

How would the children fare? She couldn't leave them if Robert's life was still in danger. An ache formed in her chest. And she couldn't bring herself to think about Dillon.

Jabali rounded the corner. "I could only find his keys."

Finding his phone in the house, like Rhysa did Lainy's, would've been too simple. If his phone wasn't in the jacket pocket, then Rhysa had to slip outside. *God, don't let him catch her.* "Where's Rhysa?"

"I'm here." Breathless, Rhysa popped into the room and closed the door. Sweat ran down her temples and stuck stray strands of hair against her neck. "It's so hot up here. I can't wait for him to leave so we can turn on the air."

"Was the phone in the truck?" Emily put a hand on both children to relish their safety.

Rhysa smiled and held out her camera. "I hope it's what you need."

Relief flooded Emily as she reached for the camera. She turned on the screen to review and saw the list of recent calls. Rhysa had taken several pictures to insure they had as much information as possible. *Smart girl.*

"See the number that starts with eight, one, six? I think that will be our man." Her hand dropped and hit the pocket of her shorts rattling something inside.

Emily's breath stalled. "Rhysa. Do you still have his keys?"

Chapter Eighteen

The color drained from Rhysa's face along with Emily's short-lived confidence. Rhysa backed up and emptied her pocket onto the bed. The keys jangled as she dropped them onto the comforter. Her hand trembled as she pulled back. "I've messed everything up."

Her doubt was contagious as it flickered across Emily's mind. Would Mark think he'd dropped his keys or would he immediately suspect the children? He did appear to have something against them. Mark's abrupt manner toward Rhysa seemed personal.

Emily considered their alternatives. Nothing seemed possible. Of course, that was because they were relying on themselves. She sucked in two deep breaths to stop the churning in her stomach and straightened her shoulders. "You haven't messed anything up. Who did we pray to before doing this, and who did we put our trust in?"

Both children answered in reply. "God."

"Right. And God will see us through." Emily grabbed the keys and with more confidence than she felt, walked toward the stairs. Worry bunched the muscles along her spine. She didn't want to come in contact with Mark. She wouldn't be able to hide the fact she knew he'd been the attacker.

Still not sure of a plan, she hoped God would direct her soon. The men hadn't left the office. Emily sighed, *thank you, Jesus.* From the top of the stairs, Mark's back was in view as well as Dillon's face. With the keys dangling from her finger, she waved them to catch Dillon's attention.

He gave an almost imperceptible nod. He knew to extend the conversation. Emily turned around. "Okay. I have an idea. Jabali—"

"I know what to do. Swing for the fences," he whispered and took the keys.

More baseball terms. Emily placed a hand over her heart. *God speed.* Jabali was brave, and probably the only solution, yet it didn't feel right to allow him to return to the lion's den. Emily and Rhysa blended into the shadows of the upstairs hall while keeping an eye on the office.

Jabali's small, light-footed figure slinked around the sofa before he dropped to a belly crawl. Without a sound, he moved toward the office with the agility of a fence lizard. Emily swallowed—he was so close. Just slip them into the—Mark dropped his arm to the side, letting it hang at the side of the chair. Unless he moved, Jabali wouldn't have access to the coat pocket.

Without time for Dillon to signal, Mark rose from his chair.

"No." Rhysa's desperate whisper matched Emily's anxious heart.

Emily squeezed her eyes shut. *Think. Think. What can we do?*

When she reopened them, Jabali was gone. Within seconds, he'd disappeared. The keys were left on the floor beside Mark's chair.

Their voices traveled past the office. "Don't get upset, Mark. I never suggested your relationship with her went beyond friendship."

"Fine. Okay." Mark tossed his jacket over his shoulder. "I'll let you know about the next convention."

As he turned to leave his foot crunched on top the keys. "Huh? Good thing I stepped on these or I wouldn't have gotten far."

Dillon followed him to the front door without comment. After closing the door, he leaned back and put a finger to his lips. Jabali appeared from the kitchen with a huge smile ready to explode.

Through the open window, Mark's truck roared to life then slowly faded down the lane. Dillon finally gave the okay. "Now we can relax!"

"Cool! Did you see me at all Uncle Dillon?" With his glass half-full attitude, Jabali had seen the whole event as something from a spy movie. "I slithered in and out like a snake."

Dillon shook his head with what appeared to be relief. "I'm just glad it's over. Good work team." He flipped the breaker in the garage and cool air shot through the vents.

"Ah." Rhysa let the air blow over her face. "Let's never have to do that again."

"I agree." Emily touched her head as she followed Dillon to the office with the camera. "Do you think Mark's on to us?"

Dillon moved toward the office and spoke low enough the children wouldn't hear. "I don't know how much he heard from the listening device before Robert destroyed it. I think it's wise to assume Mark's suspicious. The keys jingled once, but he probably thinks that's when they fell out."

"What would he do if he thought we'd set him up?" The hair on Emily's neck prickled with worry.

"I'm not sure. It's like his whole focus is on control of the business. At this point, he's capable of anything."

Dillon rubbed his temple before pointing toward the camera in Emily's hand. "Let's see if we have anything to help the police make an arrest."

"Uncle Dillon, can we hop in the pool?" Rhysa stood fanning her blouse.

"Sure. Jump in and we'll join you here in a few."

In less than five minutes, the kitchen door opened and closed drowning out the children's voices. Dillon turned to the screen. "Look. I think we found our evidence."

Emily bent closer. Rhysa had opened his texts, and listed in short increments scattered between other messages were places Robert had recently been—the places he'd been attacked. "It's time to send in a cleanup hitter." She was doing it as well. The baseball slang came out of nowhere. "Call the police."

Dillon already had his hand on the phone. Minutes ticked by as the dispatcher asked preliminary questions. Emily listened as Dillon held the phone away from his ear. The lengthy query was probably for paperwork but also stole time they didn't have.

If the evidence supported a reason for an arrest, would the information also be enough to put away the man hired to kill Robert? *God, provide the information we need. Please end this once and for all.*

"They're sending someone over."

"Good." Emily felt she could breathe again. The children would want to know, plus they were still expecting her and Dillon's company. "But I guess that cancels swimming."

"Unless you want to make a report in your bathing suit? Which I wouldn't mind except for all the attention you'd draw from the officers."

Heat rose to Emily's cheeks. Perhaps it was an escape from the adrenaline, but he'd never teased her like this before. The phone rang saving Emily from having to answer.

Dillon picked up the receiver. "Hi, Mrs. Johnson." He covered one end of the phone with his hand and whispered, "Our nosey neighbor."

"What? Weaving through your shrubs …" Dillon shot out of his chair and glimpsed out the office window. "And the truck … the police are on their way, but call and report what you saw."

Dillon grabbed Emily's hand and pulled her out the door. "Mark's on his way back."

"Did he have car trouble?"

"He's carrying a gun."

The children! They hurried through the kitchen and out the door. Emily turned and slammed into Dillon's back. He'd stopped midstride then swung his arm out to keep her from advancing.

At the edge of the pool, Mark held a gun to Rhysa's head. He yanked on her ponytail, forcing her to climb out of the water. Jabali got out by the stairs and raced toward them.

"Don't be a hero, little man. I can't wrestle both of you. So if you don't want your sister to die, back off."

"Come here, Jabali." Emily held out her arms to coax him her direction.

"You're going too far, Mark." Dillon tensed beside her. His hands rolled into tight fists. "This hole you're digging will swallow you up."

"Shut up! You should've stayed out of this." He jerked Rhysa backward by the hair.

She cried out in pain.

"Taking her won't solve anything."

"It'll keep you from calling the police. I need time, and you'll do as I tell you or this brat's gonna get it."

"Take me instead." Emily stepped forward but Dillon pulled her to a stop. She struggled against his hold trying to twist from his grip. "Let her go. She's just a child."

Mark continued to walk backwards. Rhysa's eyes darted to her surroundings. *Don't try anything, sweetie. He'll hurt you.* With another step, Mark stumbled into the outdoor furniture. He fought for balance as his foot twisted around the leg of an iron chair. Rhysa stole her opportunity. With Mark still holding tight to her ponytail, she lunged into the pool, bringing him with her.

Emily rushed forward and grabbed hold of Jabali while Dillon dove into the water. Mark broke the surface sputtering, his hands empty. He slipped under again. *Where are you Rhysa?*

At the opposite end of the pool, Rhysa swam near the bottom with the strength of a porpoise. She shot out of the water as uniformed police officers rounded the side of the house.

Water splashed and feet kicked as Dillon wrestled to keep Mark away from the gun. Mark shoved Dillon back and dove to the side. Dillon grabbed his ankle and yanked, causing a current of water to rush past Mark's head. He gasped and twisted to free himself. Dillon gave him just enough time to find his footing before clamping down on his wrist and wringing it high behind his back. Mark swung his other arm as he fought to get loose from Dillon's grip. He might have succeeded, but Dillon shoved him against the concrete side, pinning his chest to the wall.

Rhysa looked over her shoulder toward the police then pointed to the pool. "There's a gun in there. The guy in blue tried to kill me."

Emily, stunned, admired the girl's intelligence. Not only had she informed the police of the seriousness of the situation, she'd also helped them identify their culprit.

Someone blew a whistle and the water calmed. Both Dillon and Mark turned. Their eyes widened at the police officers surrounding the pool with guns drawn.

Mark eased his free hand over his head as Dillon propelled him to the edge.

An officer Emily recognized, approached Dillon.

"The gun's in the pool." Dillon pointed in the general direction. His breathing labored from the struggle with Mark.

Water poured from the men's clothes as they climbed on deck. While one officer handcuffed Mark and read him his rights, another used the net to scoop the gun from the bottom of the pool.

Rhysa ran to Emily's side and embraced her brother. Prayers had been answered. Whether the information they'd collected was enough or not, the scene the police walked into was plenty to convict. Mark would no longer be a threat.

Emily huddled with the children as the responding officer what took Dillon's statement.

Finally, the drama that had become their life was coming to a close.

***

"Let's celebrate and go out for dinner!" Dillon's announcement received a welcome round of cheers. Everyone shared his desire to get away from the house. Robert had arrived after Dillon phoned and told him of Mark's arrest. Steps were being made to arrest the hired gunman as well.

"Will Mom meet us there?" Rhysa asked her dad. Dillon hadn't called Lainy, but he assumed Robert had.

"Call and invite her. She'd like hearing from you."

Dillon glanced from one peaceful family member to the next. But where was Emily? He left the kitchen and noted the empty sitting room before starting upstairs. "Emily?"

"Up here."

He stopped in her doorway. "You okay?"

She sat on the edge of the bed, her face showed traces of tears. She turned and wiped her eyes before looking back.

"Just emotionally spent." Her attempt at a smile failed to reach her eyes. "But I have good news." She waved the cell phone in her hand as though she'd received a recent call. "My sister's getting married and wants to hold the wedding before I leave."

Dillon narrowed his eyes and dropped his gaze to the floor. Even he couldn't pretend happiness. It should've been their wedding. His and Emily's. Not knowing what else to say, he chose to change the topic. "We're getting ready to go out." He read her reluctant sigh. "And I'm not giving you the option of staying home."

Emily dragged herself to the door. The yearning to draw her into his arms planted Dillon's feet where he stood, blocking her way.

She looked up. Her brows drew together as she sighed. "We can't do that again, Dillon." Her voice grew soft with disappointment. "My heart couldn't take it."

He leaned forward as her chin dropped, and rested his forehead against hers. With one hand restraining him to the door jam, he entwined her fingers with the other. *If I told you I loved you, would you stay?* A gentle pressure kept him silent. The answer lay between her and God. With insurmountable strength, he stepped backed. His arms as empty as his chest.

***

The remaining weeks of Emily's stay drew to an end. An opportunity to talk more in-depth about her decision to leave had never presented itself. God must have given her the clarity she needed—without Dillon's consent.

He stood in front of the small bathroom mirror of his cottage and straightened his tie. He'd agreed to attend the wedding with Emily to allow her to leave the Plymouth with her parents and return with him. His chest heaved against a heavy weight. That meant he'd be the one driving her to the airport.

Two days were all they had left.

The grass around the stone path, winding between his cottage and the main house, looked more worn this year than ever before. Dillon stopped as his gaze lingered on the upstairs windows. He'd continue to wear the path down. Though he might have lost Emily, because of her, he'd gained a niece and nephew.

Rhysa met him at the door and stood back as he entered. Dressed in an ivory assemble that must have come from her mom, she stood more poised than usual.

He whistled. "You make a lovely sight, and I like your hair down."

She blushed. Something Dillon had never seen before. "Thank you. You clean up pretty good yourself."

Her quick wit never ceased to amuse him.

Jabali stopped at the kitchen entrance and gave a low bow. "Presenting, Miss Emily." He waved his arm as Emily, shaking her head, flowed into the room.

"Oh, Dillon." As if embarrassed he caught her grand entrance, she ducked her head. "I didn't expect you to be here yet."

Mesmerized, Dillon couldn't help but stare. Dressed in a classic black and white dress with her hair coiled to the side, Emily's time abroad had done nothing to dampen her sense of style.

Rhysa had told him the trouble Emily had in deciding what to buy. He cleared his dry throat. "Beautiful choice."

The children chose to ride with Emily while Dillon followed close behind. He'd never met her family. Despite the fact he and Emily were just friends, his stomach tightened.

If she weren't leaving, this could easily be their wedding a year from now. The thought wasn't new to him. When had his thinking changed? Until Emily arrived, he'd given up on the idea of marriage.

Maybe he was no longer against it because, in truth, the possibility wasn't there. She was leaving, end of story. No need to be nervous about meeting her family. No need to impress her father.

Dillon drummed his fingers against the steering wheel and stared at the road.

After an hour of driving, the malls and housing that crowded the highway gave way to a scattering of businesses among forested hills. Although beautiful, decked in their full green foliage, the area also reminded him of where he'd been shot.

His thoughts trailed back to the fall. Robert could have found the deer trail in half the time, but Dillon had finally located an area that promised frequent crossing and settled into position to wait. The temperature that day had dropped fifteen degrees, stealing much of the enjoyment from the hunt. After an hour or two of no movement his limbs had grown stiff and achy.

Just as he'd risen the first blast exploded. Even now as he thought back to the moment, a searing pain throbbed deep within his shoulder. The next thing he'd remembered was Emily's voice.

His loss of blood, coupled with dehydration had caused him to hallucinate. Emily, he'd thought, was an angel sent from above. And for the last four months, it had seemed she was.

***

"So you're Dillon Brewington."

Dillon shook the offered hand of Ethan Durham, Emily's oldest brother. His serious gaze took in Dillon with alarming scrutiny. Didn't he realize there wasn't a reason for sizing him up? His sister was leaving.

"I hope Ethan isn't making a pest of himself." A tall, slender blonde stopped by Ethan's side. "I'm Carli, his wife. He has a way of being a little protective of those he loves."

"He's fine. Nothing I wouldn't do."

Ethan's gaze relaxed. A common thread in life was often all it took to start a friendship.

Emily arrived with her mom, Rhysa, and Jabali. "The kids love the farm. I wish I would've found the time to bring them out here before."

Dillon admired the rosy hue brightening her face. She was happy and relaxed, surrounded by family. A selfish pang tightened his chest. Before he could think past his self-pity Ann patted his arm.

"We all want you to know you're welcome here any time. And I appreciate you doing this for Emily. I'm much more comfortable knowing she won't be driving back to the city in that old car. But if I told her that she wouldn't listen."

"Mom, I'm standing right here."

"It's my pleasure, Mrs. Durham." Dillon enjoyed being a part of their interactions.

"I told you its Ann. Mrs. Durham makes me sound far too serious." She turned at the sound of stringed instruments being tuned. "I think we'd better take our seats."

Emily motioned for them to follow her brother and sister-in-law toward the rows of seating.

Dillon eyed the wooden folding chair. The aged design appeared to be built for much smaller frames.

Emily's younger brother, Keaton Durham, whispered from one row back. "Don't worry. I haven't had one break beneath me yet."

Dillon looked back to the chair and took his seat. The family had greeted him with warmth and respect, and he didn't want it to change by collapsing the chair during the middle of the wedding.

Emily glanced at him from the corner of her eye. He pretended not to notice. It wasn't the first time he'd caught her staring. A good sign, he hoped.

Seated in front of him, one of Ethan's sons looked over his dad's shoulder. Dillon glanced from him to the identical twin in his mother's lap. Double the trouble. The first twin smiled widely then let go a strand of unintelligible words.

As an aunt, Emily was definitely blessed. Counting the new step-daughter this marriage would add, there were nine grandchildren in the Durham family. Having only Robert to contend with growing up, Dillon couldn't imagine what gatherings would be like with a family this size. He scanned the crowd of happy faces—fun and eventful.

A small, bluegrass band started up the wedding march. Dillon smiled and eased off the less-than-trusted chair to stand. The outdoor setting, coupled with the music gave an air of stepping back in time.

Emily's sister, Lucy, held onto her dad's arm with one hand while the other clutched a bouquet of wild flowers. The man she was to marry stood near the pastor with eyes that never left his bride.

Dillon swallowed and struggled to maintain enjoyment over the event. The white haired pastor said a few words before the vows, stressing their importance.

Knowing he faced rejection, Dillon slipped his hand over Emily's. He felt the jolt of her surprise. Like a starched glove, her hand stilled for several moments before relaxing in his. Whether she liked it or not, he intended to make it clear that when she left, she'd be taking a part of him with her.

Chapter Nineteen

Emily stopped beside Robert while he deposited her bag by the door.

"You pack light for a woman, but I guess that's due to all your traveling."

"It's a humbling experience when you realize how little the majority have in the world."

"Then after the time you've spent here, you probably think I'm as affluent as they come."

"Not at all. You've shown you can be faithful with a few things so God's blessed you with more."

Robert held her gaze. His eyes shined with admiration. "This house won't be the same without you."

Dillon opened the door from the garage. "The car's cooled and ready."

Emily turned back to Rhysa and Jabali. Leaving had never hurt this much. Her heart felt as if it would shatter. Jabali rushed into her arms. "I love you, Emily."

She bent to her knees. "I love you, too. And remember, I promise to write."

Rhysa tucked a stray strand of hair behind her ear and moved closer. Something was written on her palm.

Emily stood and took Rhysa's hand. Blue letters spelled the name, "Emily."

A sob broke from Rhysa's throat. "I-I won't forget you."

Emily made it to the car before the dam broke. She huddled against the window to hide the worst of her emotions from Dillon. How could leaving the children be right when it felt so wrong?

Miles passed by unseen. Exhausted and numb, she reached for a clean tissue and blotted her eyes. Finding her voice, she forced herself to ask, "Will the children be all right?"

Dillon's chest expanded with his intake of air. "None of us will be the same." He took her hand in his. The warmth of his touch seared a deep inner ache.

A new floodgate of tears pressed against her lids. *God, give me strength.*

They arrived at the airport. Emily checked her luggage then turned to Dillon. "We both know I have a long wait. Please go ahead and leave. It'll be easier that way."

A muscle throbbed in Dillon's jaw. His eyes explored hers, revealing his pain. "I—None of this is easy." He took her hand and she allowed him to lead her to a row of seats.

Emily waited for him to say more. His defeated posture plainly stated what was left unsaid. He couldn't risk revealing his heart and add to the pressure she'd already piled on herself. That reason alone was enough to make her love him—only she already did.

They held hands in silence until the last boarding call was made. Emily handed in her ticket. It would only take a moment. One small crack in her thin veneer of strength and she'd be in his arms. He'd hold her tight.

Whisper she shouldn't go. Promise to love her. And …
she'd live in regret for ignoring God's call.

Emily boarded the plane and found her seat number
next to the window. She lifted the shade with tentative
fingers. Dillon was no doubt still inside. Waiting until
the plane was gone from sight. Leaving him was the
hardest decision she'd ever made in her life.

Guilt mingled with devotion. The final plans to the
mission had never cleared. Each time she tried to pray
for clarity her thoughts would jumble, dwelling on the
Brewington children, her family, and of course,
lingering on Dillon, where they'd become stuck.

***

With her pack lighter, Emily no longer fought to
keep it on her shoulder. She'd given out more Bibles
and pamphlets in Kurdistan in one day than in any of
her other mission trips. Although most of the Kurds
claimed to be Muslim, many listened to Emily and the
others in her evangelist group and eagerly accepted
anything they offered. The harvest truly was plentiful.

She left a juice stand after sharing with three young
Kurds and swallowed the last of the drink she'd
purchased. A man, waving his arms, ran across the
street toward them. Emily shared a quick glance with
her fellow missionaries. They'd been prepped for
trouble, but had yet to feel any hostility. *God, speak
through us.*

He stopped at her feet and gulped for air, his anxiety
evident, as he hadn't run far. "I want one." He pointed
to the pack on her shoulder then behind him to the
store across the street. A man stood outside the shop
and waved. Emily recognized him from the night
before. He'd been present in a meeting they'd held in a
Kurdish believer's home.

Her sigh of relief mingled with those around her. "Of course." She reached into her pack and withdrew a study Bible.

The man brought it to his lips and kissed the cover. "Ah, the Sword of the Spirit."

Shame weighed on Emily's heart. She'd half-hoped her presence wouldn't be needed in Kurdistan and that she'd misunderstood God, but the numerous opportunities to share the gospel stated the opposite.

"Time to head back." Someone from her group waved for a taxi.

Emily pulled herself from her thoughts and glanced at her watch. It was time to catch the ferry.

Two weeks had passed and Emily's stubborn heart still hadn't accepted her new position with peace. Leaving Tatvan, she and the other missionaries crossed Lake Van to return to their host families. She fanned a slip of paper in front of her as hot air slipped through an opened door.

Out the window, billowing clouds spread across the sky in splendor. Still, they failed to thrill her as in times past. *God, where's my joy? Isn't this what You wanted?* A soft wind rippled the lake's surface. She closed her eyes and imagined the cool water tickling the sensitive hollow behind her ankles. Memories of times spent at the creek soothed her mind then switched to those of swimming with Rhysa and Jabali.

She missed home.

The unbidden confession shook her. She'd never battled adjustment this hard. Here, unlike in the United States, life moved at a slower pace. People took time to listen. Serving overseas had always offered solace for Emily. Why not now?

She turned to the young Italian volunteer seated beside her. "What made you want to help the Kurds?"

Francesca looked up from the planner in her lap. Her brown eyes implored Emily to explain.

"Why here and not somewhere else? How did you know this was God's will for your life?"

"Oh, I see." She cocked her head to the side in thought. "I had other jobs, but the situation with the Kurds pulled at my heart."

Could it be that easy? Had she only to follow her heart—that would lead her back to Dillon! "So you followed where your heart led you?"

"Not exactly." Francesca smiled. "I prayed, of course."

Emily's moment of elation stalled. "But how did God answer so you knew you should come here?"

She waved a hand in the air as if swatting a gnat. "Simple. He said, 'Francesca, if you want to go to Kurdistan then empty your hands.'"

Her eyes softened with compassion at the confusion Emily knew blanketed her face. "He means I stop my other jobs. He likes what I do in Italy. But He also says this is good. I get to choose. And when I finally make up my mind, I am rewarded with complete peace."

Emily struggled to wrap her mind around the simplicity of Francesca's words.

She patted Emily's arm. "Do not struggle so hard with what God's will is for *your* life. Just follow *His* will. Simple."

"But ... I thought I was supposed to work with the Kurds. I'm spreading God's message. That is His will."

"You remember Philip, mentioned in Acts? He had a very powerful few years. Later, all scripture mentions about him is he raised four virgin daughters that did prophecy. Like Philip, you've served God faithfully on the front line, but now He may have need of you in a different area."

Emily slowly nodded in awe of Francesca's wisdom.

"Your heart is somewhere else, no?" Her accented words broke through Emily's concentration. "I think God can use you either place. But He will get the most out of you where your heart is." She smiled. "And maybe you, too, will find peace."

***

Because of an accident on the road, Dillon arrived too late to accompany his dad to lunch. The nurse mentioned he'd been given a tray of food. At least he'd eaten.

A chair sat near the bed. Dillon pulled it closer and watched as his dad fought to stay awake. Faded blue eyes widened slightly in recognition of company then rolled back beneath heavy lids.

If he were healthy and sound of mind, what advice would he give? Snapshots of his parents together filtered through Dillon's mind. His mother would've loved Emily. She would've seen straight through to her heart and been excited to have her as a daughter-in-law.

He glanced back at his dad. No doubt, he'd just be happy if Dillon was happy. Always the romantic, Dad never failed to jump on board when his sons thought they were in love. It was Dillon's mom who voiced common sense about the girls they chose.

Dillon clasped his dad's aged hand in his and noted the crook in his ring finger. He ran his thumb over the knotted bone and remembered the summer it was broken. Unaware of his strength as a young teen, Dillon had cracked the bat against Robert's fastball, breaking his dad's finger as he caught it.

An inner warmth lifted his mood. Although he'd always felt guilty over swinging so hard, his dad had beamed with pride.

Dad's hand tightened around Dillon's. His tired eyes blinked as he fought for focus. "Hi, Son. Where's that pretty girl you've been keeping company with?"

Dillon held his breath afraid a wrong move might disrupt his dad's strong frame of mind. "She's …" How did he answer and not disappoint his dad or cause his mind to relapse? "She's working." The answer slipped past his lips.

Dad nodded and closed his eyes again. "Just be sure to bring her back."

Dillon swallowed. *Wouldn't I like to.* His dad had no idea how complicated his idea was, but one Dillon had given plenty of thought to.

I'll go to the ends of the world for her, God, if that's what You want. Just give me confirmation.

***

In the shop, Dillon knocked over the flux as he drew his brush back. He sighed and stared at the mess. The day wasn't going as planned.

Jabali sauntered in through the front door and tossed his backpack on the floor. He evidently hadn't stopped at the house. Both children avoided being inside since Emily left.

Dillon grabbed a towel to wipe up his spill. "Bad day or good day?"

Jabali dragged a stool next to his and shrugged. "Does it matter?" He picked up a piece of stained glass and began wrapping the copper foil around the edge. Less than a month of working with Dillon and he already knew what to do without instruction. "I still miss Emily."

Didn't they know it wasn't easy for him either? "I didn't say you wouldn't. I said you'd get used to her being gone." Dillon rubbed his temple.

"But I'm not!" Jabali had never raised his voice at his uncle.

Dillon let his action slide without rebuke. He understood all too well. "I'm not used to it either."

"Then bring her back." Rhysa appeared behind them with her hands on her hips.

Dillon didn't move and barely breathed. Could this be the confirmation he'd asked for?

"Yeah, bring her back." Jabali agreed.

Chapter Twenty

Turkey, Iran, Kurdistan, all blended into one very hot, arid place. Dillon disembarked the ferry, amazed he'd made it this far. A guide dressed in slacks and a button-down, long-sleeved shirt, directed him in choppy English to a taxi that would take him to the mission school.

He settled into the sweltering cab and was thrown against the back seat. Another thing he recently learned, all taxis in Kurdistan drove at the same speed—very fast.

They left the city of Van and took a dusty road over hillsides of barren land. A hypnotic melody played over the radio. The ambient stringed instrument and vocalist might have succeeded in lulling Dillon to sleep if not for his mounting anticipation.

His heart quickened as a cluster of battered gray and ocher walls appeared up ahead. To his knowledge, Emily didn't expect him. Would she be willing to leave?

Tommy Donavan, the one Emily referred to as her uncle, had tried to contact her. His job was easier than Dillon's. He simply had to call. Had she heard from him yet? Dillon hoped so, as it would make her decision that much easier.

If she could've talked to Tommy before leaving, she may have never left at all. The new division of his organization concentrated on building relations with Kurds in St. Louis in hopes of sharing the message of salvation. And Tommy felt Emily should direct it.

What irony.

The cab pulled to a stop. The dust settled as Dillon paid the driver. The village seemed to emerge out of nowhere. Surrounded by desert, the ragged buildings looked like a deserted town.

"Dillon?" Emily's familiar voice washed over him in a blanket of warmth. He turned from the side of the road unable to seize his thoughts. Like a vision from his dreams, Emily stood outside a rough tin building. Her braided hair hung against a white shirt. Children bumped against her as they emerged from the schoolhouse, pushing her forward.

His smile started in his heart and spilled outward. He was here to bring her home. As if she understood, Emily's dropped jaw morphed into a huge grin. The clipboard fell from her hand as she ran toward him.

He captured her in his arms and held her tight against his chest.

Dream or not, Dillon wasn't about to let go. Her nearness caused a surge of joy to well up inside his heart. He swung her around, her laughter rippling through the air like the sweetest song in the world.

Emily pressed her cheek against his and whispered in disbelief, "I can't believe you're here."

"I'd go to the end of the world for you, Emily." He set her down absorbing every feature in her pretty face.

A light-hearted laugh tumbled from her throat. "I believe you have." Questions formed in her eyes as she stared at him. How long should he hold on to the moment before explaining his presence?

She answered his thoughts with hope in her voice. "Have you come to take me home?" An exuberant joy sparkled in her luminous gaze.

Dillon's heart skipped several beats. "Yes, and I'm not giving you the option of staying."

She laughed again and moved closer. "Well, you certainly couldn't leave me. My heart couldn't take being separated from you again."

A chorus of giggles rose from their audience. A helper tried, without success, to corral the children back inside.

Dillon chuckled at the scene they made. "Have you heard from your Uncle Tommy?" He rubbed her braid in his hand wanting to seal everything about her in his heart.

She hung her head with mock shame. "Yes. And I suppose you already know what he had to say?" She looked up and continued after his nod. "If only I'd taken the time to call him back, everything would have been clear. Yes, the Kurds had been put on my heart for a reason. I just didn't have to go so far to help."

Dillon took her hand and directed their attention back to the school. "Something tells me your trip here still had purpose." Children giggled and whispered amongst themselves.

Emily turned serious eyes toward him. "What about Rhysa and Jabali? Do they know you're here?"

"They're the ones who told me to go." Dillon relished the look of surprise. Her freckled nose turned a light shade of pink as a sheen of tears covered her eyes.

Emily wrapped her arms around him again. "Thank you for coming for me. I won't leave you ever again."

"Promise?"

Emily pulled back to look him in the eye. "Promise." The seriousness of her tone answered the question he had yet to ask.

He pulled a box from his pocket and glanced at the children. Smiles he didn't think could widen stretched tighter across their faces. A worker with dark hair motioned for him to bend to his knees. His mouth pulled to the side. *As if I needed told.*

With one knee on the ground, he opened the box toward Emily. "Will you marry me?" Four simple words that held a lifetime of meaning.

"Yes!" Emily clasped her hands to her face and batted tears as they threatened to fall. "I love you, Dillon."

He stood and pulled her into his arms. His throat thickened with emotion. "I love you, too."

She sighed against him as he closed his eyes. He heard the cheer of his youthful crowd. No more striking out, he'd finally made a home run.

###

A Note from the Author

I knew I wanted to focus on prayer before I ever started Devoted Mission. Prayer is the mightiest tool we have as Christians, yet one greatly overlooked—just as spiritual battle often is. If we could all train ourselves to wake and ask God, "Strengthen me for the battle I'm stepping into today," and pray His armor for ourselves, family and friends, think how much easier our day might go. I hope Emily and Dillon's story has given you food for thought and may you leave here stronger than before.

Two years prior to finishing this novel, God pressed on my heart to draw attention to the Kurdish people. It is my prayer that someone reading this will be encouraged to follow the path God has been directing you toward.

Thank you for reading Devoted Mission. Please consider leaving a review at your favorite online store. Your encouraging words could be the catalyst someone else needs to purchase this book. Not only would you be sharing the Godly messages I shared with you, but you would also help promote me as an author.

Stay connected with me by liking The Ozark Durham Series on Facebook and by signing up for my news-letter at www.reginatittel.com.

Thanks again, and God bless!

Regina